M

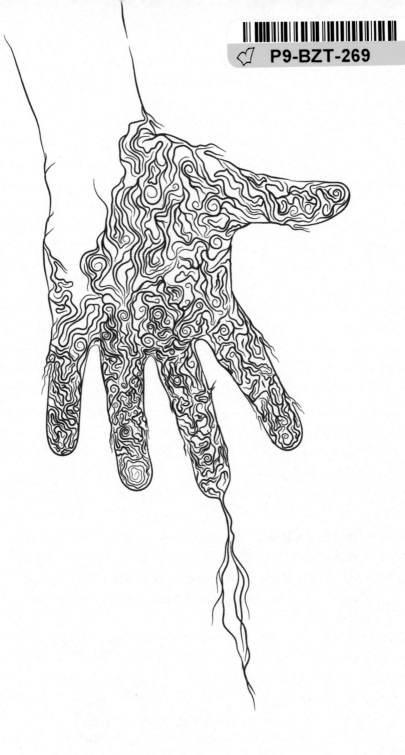

Fiction
Bosko. D

Broken Eye Books is an independent press, here to bring you the odd, strange, and offbeat side of speculative fiction. Our stories tend to blend genres, blurring the boundaries of sci-fi, weird, and fantasy, and mixing in elements of horror and other genres.

Support weird. Support indie.

brokeneyebooks.com

twitter.com/brokeneyebooks
facebook.com/brokeneyebooks

NEVER NOW ALWAYS

DESIRINA BOSKOVICH

NEVER NOW ALWAYS
by DESIRINA BOSKOVICH
Published by
Broken Eye Books
www.brokeneyebooks.com

Copyright © 2017 Broken Eye Books and Desirina Boskovich
Cover design by Jeremy Zerfoss
Interior design and editing by Scott Gable, C. Dombrowski,
and Matt Youngmark

ISBN-10: 1-940372-27-5
ISBN-13: 978-1-940372-27-3

Never Now Always
Desirina Boskovich

001
(lolo)

THERE IS A NOW WHERE CARETAKERS COME DOWN.

Sometimes, it happens in the park. Us sisters run and call through blotchy grass and tight-packed earth. We soar on swings with creaking, rasping chains. We streak down the rust-marred slide, descend on jagged bolts and itchy steel.

We jump rope beneath the maple trees.

We dare each other—*Leap from the swing!*—and we sail through the sky like things with wings before crashing on all fours into the faded wood chips.

The trash barrel stinks of rotting candy and swarms with wicked bees.

This now, the sky goes gray, and clouds press in. The fog swirls and the mist subdues.

My sister's hand now slips away. The world is hazy, and then it's not; now me, Lolo, in the dark. The wind lashes my cheeks and whips my hair across bared teeth while the swings shriek in the breeze.

The sound is my terror: metal on metal, clanking chains, the groaning creak, the dying wheeze.

I can't see my hand for the mist. My sister calls my name. I call hers (a name I can't just now recall). Grass crushed by wind. I fall to ground, lie flat against the bark, my cheek to dirt.

The darkness clears, mist recedes, and from foggy nothing steps this Caretaker, the very first I see.

For a moment, it shimmers, like it is resolving into something. It has no ears. It has no mouth; it cannot speak. It possesses eyes alone, sunk into a pale orb of a head.

As the mist clears, I scream. The distant labyrinth is growing, built but incomplete, a skeleton against the sky.

I clench my fingers against my sweat-slick palm, the sticky shadow of my sister's grip.

The memory departed, I'm in the room again. Strapped in a chair I can't decamp. My ankles bound, my wrists secured, my chest braced. The spotlight glaring in my eyes.

Two Caretakers stake out one corner, ahead and to my right. Silent, they observe. I search out their eyes. I see them, they see me, but our gazes can't connect.

The room speaks in its voice. "What happened?"

I always answer. Something bad occurs if I refuse. Just now, I can't remember what. But I know I answer always *or else* . . . or else *something*. That something, it's enough.

I like to please the Voice.

"The Caretakers come."

"For the first time?" The voice is womanish, doctor-sounding, speaking clear and distant, like she's very close and far at once.

"Yes. For the first time."

"How did you feel when you saw one?"

"I feel afraid."

"Did they hurt you?"

"No."

"So why did you feel afraid?"

"I can't find my sister."

"There is no sister. What did it feel like when you were lying with your cheek against the rubber turf?"

It comes over me, like a wave. How I am alone in the park. I remember the springy slack of turf, the soft rubber's earnest smell. How the indentations wobble as my fingers grasp while my heart hammers against the trembling ground.

The bloodless sky rips open with another story.

The Voice asks.

I answer.

The Caretakers watch with dead, dark eyes.

"Gor?" I say.

"Lolo?" says Gor.

I'm above. Gor below. We speak in whispers. It is dark. It is night. We rest in stacked bunks inside our sleeping pod.

"What was before?" I ask, knowing even as I say the words they're wrong. The words I need aren't real or are still unknown. This titanic notion waits lodged inside my chest like an air bubble that won't pop. My thought can't hatch.

"Before what?" Gor says.

"Before now."

"Breakfast," Gor says, first faltering and then bold. "Breakfast."

There are words that mean time: *before, after, next, yesterday, tomorrow, morning, night.* We're shaky with such words.

Space, space is simple. We know *left* and *right*, *up* and *down*, *in* and *out*, *above* and *below*. We think in the shape of our dwelling maze.

Time speech is harder. We retain too many holes; we miss too much.

I want to ask things. I can't recall the words I need. Sometimes, most times, I can't think what the question is at all.

I contemplate. Is *breakfast* a word for time? No. A word for food. But also time. Food and time, intertwined.

"No," I contradict. "Not breakfast."

"Why not? I like breakfast."

"Because it's night."

"Yes. It's night."

"Breakfast is morning." This fact I know pat, got all figured out. But breakfast is only adjacent to the real question and not close at that.

This is what they call, *You're getting colder.*

"I do like breakfast."

In darkness, I cast my gaze upward. Guilty for this private eye roll, I lean past my bunk's edge, inspect Gor upside-down.

At night, the walls glow midnight blue. Other beady, greenish lights flicker *dot-dash* along straight lines. The stillness is a stagnant hush of rustles, whirs, beeps, and breaths, the murmur of rapt children's dreams and all-the-time aloof machines.

"Can I come down, Gor?"

"Yes."

I know him because together we sleep in this bubble—always me above, always him below. I know him; he knows me. I'm Lolo; he's Gor. These facts are also pat.

I crawl from my bunk and climb down the ladder. Creep stealth-like into blankets, ally myself with him. He swaddles me in sheets that stink of clean and breezes me with his own hot breaths. His fingers warm, his toes cold. My back to him, his front to me.

"I mean *before*. More before. Before the bunk. Before the bubble. Before breakfast."

His shrug nudges my shoulder. His laugh tickles moistly at my neck. "I'm sleepy, Lolo. Because it's night."

"We'll sleep," I say. "Soon." *Another word for time is* soon.

"Because it's night."

"I can't remember."

"So sleep," Gor says.

Doing as he recommends, we close eyes, cease whispers, and forget all mystery. We wander into sleep.

Gor, he likes breakfast. Me, I like Gor.

Gor likes me, and all rapt children like breakfast.

We sit in brightness 'round the slick white table while the walls glow yellow for morning times. The children around us are chattering and hushed. They speak of memories and dreams.

Some children have shared recollections, and through eager theories, they contrive a fable. But there are those whose remembrances are their own alone. When they try to weave a tale, the others look away, hurt and confused, until all fall silent and the thread wends back to lore that's shared.

I don't speak my visions. I am Lolo, and I listen only, forever and always, canny and quiet . . . like the forest deer. (The image comes unbidden, born from somewhere: fragile, bright-eyed creature, brooding in the brush.)

The Voice calls, one by one, the number of each rapt child. Our numbers are etched into our thoughts like a tattoo within the skin. When we hear our number, we cannot help but move. By this passcode to our thoughts and limbs, we jerk instinctively to life. Like an electric tingle that teaches, but this one feels good. Like I like to please the Voice, I like to come when my number is called.

(Our names are different. Our names are our own, birthed from some primal place like a whimper in the night.)

I walk to my cubby and press my fingers to the door. The glass slides open, and inside is the three-part tray, the fodder always three different lurid colors.

Gor gets extra. Gor is always hungry.

Gor smacks his lips and licks his sticky fingers while children theorize how the labyrinth was built especially for us in the skeleton of a passed-away world. After my remembrance yesterday, I know the truth. But I do not say a word. I hold it, I touch it, I turn it over, I clutch it close to my chest like a stolen, precious thing.

It is hard to hear of others' dreams.

The Caretakers stand motionless at the four corners, eyes like black marbles with swiveling scope. They do not eat. Their presence is a darkness. We fear them, but they have been with us always, and we need them, too.

The Voice pronounces my number for lab mission. I abandon my deconstructed morsels, quite resistible. (Sometimes the food changes shape or color as we try to eat. I'm not sure what it is.) Anyway, all hunger is forgotten in my rising panic of memory duty. I'm afraid to remember and more afraid of all I do not know.

The Voice is my mistress. My number is my ruler. I come when it calls.

I'm in the room.

The Caretakers point silently at the chair where I take in times past. I am Lolo, a rapt child, and obedient, I sit. I rest my feet upon the ledge, my wrists upon the ridge, and the chair binds me fast in tethers like slithering snakes, what the Voice calls my safety restraints.

This chair is warm and tender. I am molded in its grip. It shifts for me and almost sucks me in. It's almost like there's no chair there? I'm comfortable but cannot move an inch.

Then the Caretakers sidle close. Their raspy robes scratch the edges of my hands. Their damp cool fingers almost touch my cheeks as they check my chains. They smell of mushrooms and soil after rain.

These descriptions are from times past. The labyrinth holds no such odors, no soggy sights, no dripping sounds. These eerie fragments rise from memories I cannot reach—all forgotten but the body's sense of things.

One Caretaker pushes a science cart near me, laden with instruments of trials. I watch trembling as they choose a syringe, fill it, tap the needle's dripping point. One moves close, the other at my other side. I cannot move. I squeeze my eyes tight shut. I feel it pierce against my neck, the queasy liquid glugging in. For an instant, their potion stings and burns.

I am altered. The room swivels and shifts.

Roused and impaired, I submit to this story of another now.

This time, I'm in some foreign city, unbeknownst to me until now. Walls like mazes, gray and concrete; streets of cobbled stone. Burnt out wrecks of metal. Barbed wire rolling, like tumbleweeds in breeze.

This sound makes me afraid: the rasping metal burs, scratching against the stone.

All is light and noise and wind. My thin scrap of dress is torn, dirty, bloodied, and whipping in the gale. Indistinctly, there's roaring overhead. Then the wail of sirens, a shriek that rises and falls like a wobbling wheel; it rises and falls, but never ends. A voice chants endless warning static over broken speakers.

I look up into the narrow space of sky between two towers. There, in pale white sky, I see their ships, black silhouettes. Shaped like saucers. Shaped like cigars. Shaped like snowflakes.

I stand, buffeted by breeze, almost falling, and brace my palm against the building near. The rough of granite scratches palms.

I look around, quite panicked. My sister was just here.

We were together. And now she's gone.

I turn in slow rotation and frantic, call her name. A name I can't remember.

A name I can't know. Nor can I even hear myself above the roar and shriek and wind and the endless warning voice. So her name remains unknown.

As I move in slow ballet, calling all directions, I stop dead still. There in the alley is a rushing flood, and it flows so fast toward me, a river of swirling, churning blood.

I stumble back. I can't outpace it, so I stand there as it overcomes, and on it flows. I am here, to my ankles in blood.

And now, above the other sounds, I hear the shrills of screaming kids.

This idea comes from somewhere—I don't know where.

I bend and bow down low. I dip my finger in the pool of blood. I draw one stroke against the granite wall. And then another. I'm writing a message: *I love you. I'll find you. I'll see you in Paris.*

Somehow, my vision pulls back—perhaps, I'm caught in the wave of blood—and I see the wall is the size of the world: a million messages, penned and scrawled in desperate longing by every sister and brother and forlorn cousin. This endless wall is filled with infinite graffiti to those who forget or are forgotten.

I won't forget.

I won't forget.

Then, coming toward me, the Harvesters. More clanking, rasping metal. They hulk and splash and pace inexorably toward me, to take me apart, to swallow the useful parts, to spit out the rest. I'm backing up, I'm backing up. It's not enough. The arm of the Harvester reaches to pin me. I understand the source of blood.

The room again.

I'm hoarse from screams. My back is wet from pooling sweat.

I'm holding this to me: this feel of writing, my fingertip's wet journey . . . how blood and body come together to leave words behind. I didn't know I knew such things.

If I could move, I'd pinch myself and secure the memory in pain. Instead, I grit my teeth against forgetting, grind my jaw to force back loss. I strive to hold—in the muscles of my wrists and the space behind my eyes. I hold the feeling. How it felt to form those words, how I used my gesture to make a mark that might survive.

I hold this to me. I hold it close.

The Voice speaks. "Where were you this time?"

"I'm in a city. A place I don't recognize."

"Did you know where you were?"

"I don't remember."

"Were you alone?"

"My sister . . ."

"Were you with your sister?"

"Maybe. I think I feel someone beside me. But when I turn around, no one is there."

"What did she look like?"

"I . . . um." I struggle hard through broken memories, through disjointed synapses. I try to bring it to mind. A face like mine, but different? A smile that crinkles around the edges just before it starts. An expression in the eyes. Anything.

I can't reach it. The Caretakers watch me with their empty faces. They gaze from pale expanse of nothing. Nothing below the eyes but four quivering slits that might be how they hear or how they smell or how they breathe?

"I can't remember."

"Maybe she wasn't there after all?"

"Maybe . . ."

"So you were alone?"

"Maybe."

"What did the alley look like?"

It goes like this, on and on. The Voice speaks. I answer. The Voice questions. I answer. The Voice pokes and pushes and prods, points me to some vision I can't quite fathom. The same questions, altered slightly, just a bit. Sometimes, the same words again, which feels like a trick.

I falter, unsure. I tell it again. The Voice sounds satisfied, or perhaps, I only imagine it so, dreaming a feeling for a machine person with no such feels.

I am distracted these times, thinking only of what it could mean to make words like that, words that remain. To leave a story that, whatever else is lost, the story stays. I handle this curiosity, and my thoughts are wild and bold.

Meanwhile, the Voice speaks on, and I answer—and answer more 'til my mouth is parched desert-dry. (From somewhere, a stretch of fractal-cracked earth.) The Caretakers drip water on my tongue, like to a wee hamster in a cage.

The Voice asks me of the wall, and I describe it best I can: a boundless harum-scarum scrawl of "Find me," "Find you," "Have you seen," "I'll meet you," "Lost," "Missing," "Found," like a history of the world.

The Caretakers draw near again, cautious as they always are, though, of course, there's little I can do restrained so.

They inject my veins once more, but this fluid is a sudden rush of joy. I lean lolling against the seat from which I cannot anyhow stir or stray, and I let the warm wash over me, like gold and liquid light.

Again, the Voice asks, and I retell a story of blood and screams and harvest that now feels oddly lightened in my heart because how can there be such loss and terror when I am fixed here in the light?

I begin to conjure this story in the moment of my mind.

I dream of a time such that I could write. As I did in nows like that one. As I did to leave a message, some feels or thoughts that could survive.

This is how I grasp the thread that takes me from this now until a time I cannot see.

I have these thoughts. And in my dream, these blissful thoughts that I could write again, scrawl such messages . . . all is coming clear this now, next now, all time, forever. I'll record this now, so next time I ask about before, it all appears . . .

Bumping and bobbling against this thought comes the next, just as quick but sharp: if I write, I must have blood.

If I write, I must have blood.

The Voice carps and worries on, and in my golden state, I recount past horrors. Before the Caretakers came the Harvesters, clomping and stomping with earth-shaking strength along all streets, snatching and stealing any shrieking signs of life. This I know. This I remember. Such things I could not know before, but I know them now, and I tell it with . . . with *boredsom* bliss, still floating on the fluid.

But beneath these illusions, I am me, somewhere far but almost touchable, still Lolo. And sneaky, I begin to plot with wily cunning—how to find the blood I seek.

Such blood could only be my own.

I have a thought of blades, of science instruments like on the cart. This cart

I cannot reach. I am still bound. Yet all memory duties must come to an end as all questioning sessions. So as I speak through raptured fog, I keep close eye on these torment gadgets. Same time, I see the Caretakers keep close eye on me, but I refuse all fear.

Our talking on-and-on is interrupted by a wailing turmoil. The room blares and squawks and shakes while lights flash a blue-to-yellow revolution. I sense I know this sound and what it signifies, but I can remember nothing of it. I know only a cold and creeping dread that almost breaks the bliss.

The Caretakers move quick to a panel upon the wall, sheltered from my sight.

This alarm is too loud for my tender hearing, too bright for my sheltered eyes, and it crackles hair-raised against my painful skin.

We live most times in gentle light and mild air and serenely yielding floors. This is not that. I writhe and tremble against the blitz.

Then I know: this brief, din-drenched instance, I am a moment freed. My restraints are unlocked and cast aside.

Still bound by languid burnout, my futile muscles are weakened by the drug. I fight to move. I reach first with my mind to scrabble upon the other side. This battle is submerged, fought somewhere low within my muddled mind. It is a skirmish buried deep.

While the Caretakers fiddle and tinker in their silent, nasty way at controls I cannot see, I feel a screaming panic, almost near enough to reach. Take it. The syringe. I tell myself, *Do it now. Reach. Try.*

I reach first for the feeling (fear, love, anger, loss—it is written in scrawls on that infinite wall). *Reach. Try.*

I reach for the syringe.

For the briefest moment, I hold it in my palm and then tuck it deep and hidden in my sleeve.

The brightness in my eyes recedes, the wail becomes a whine, and the Caretakers abandon their secret task upon the console. They are unspeaking as always.

The tethers bind themselves against my wrists once more.

Our peculiar labyrinth sometimes spasms in weeping fits and moody outbursts of its own.

It came so slowly yet so quickly. I almost cannot fathom it happened as a fact.

I think perhaps 'twas only a hallucination, a lucid delusion, one verse or chapter in this waking dream.

I think I thought to move my hand and yet was still.

I think I *visioned* this cold danger against the pale lifelines of my palm, yet it remains on the science cart, undisturbed. The things I think exist are seldom real.

Yet I feel it still within my sleeve. An intrusion, cold and steel. It waits.

I also wait. Knowing, cold and cunning and not at all afraid, that this now is not the same as nows before. This now has changed.

Soon.

Another word for time is *soon.*

Night comes. I lie quiet in my bunk, breathing as steady as any rapt child who's forgotten before's nightmares.

"Lolo?" Gor says from below, but I pretend to sleep.

Soon, he's sleeping, too. I listen and breathe, awash in his snuffling snores.

In this bubble, he is my courage, my heart. He doesn't know what I'm about to do. I didn't tell him. I wouldn't dare. I lie here, my chest beating fast. I am afraid.

I am *very* afraid.

But pain is just pain. It is fleeting. It is always forgotten. It can be fought.

Gor murmurs in his sleep. Crying out in the flicker of befores that might be our own—or maybe not.

I rummage in the hollow at the side of my bunk and produce my stolen good. I sit up, inspect its fierce, sharp prick in the greenish flicker that *luminates* all nights.

I grit my teeth against my tears and yelps and clench my jaw tight shut. In the pallid softness of my forearm, like the serpent's underbelly, I plunge the needle.

Pain is just pain.

I scratch and drag. I make the first cut.

With the needle's honed point, I etch the first tremulous symbol against the gray wall above my bunk. I inscribe it tiny. I cannot already know the size of this splintered and perplexing story, but I know my ink is hard won, and my canvas is not in endless supply.

The first symbol is a swing set.

One frame, two swings. One for each sister.

I've forgotten letters, I've forgotten words. If I sit very still and hold my feeling to myself, I can almost remember how it felt to shape them. Or rather, the feels they gave: some clarity, some truth, something not vague. But their forms are lost to me. Their contours, their silhouettes, their downward lines and horizontal strokes. Gone. Lost to some before.

I trace a swing.

More cuts. More blood. More jaw-clenched tears.

I trace a cloud.

More cuts. More breath.

I sketch a blurry portrait of a Harvester, the creepy-crawly limbs that reach and grasp.

I draw a wall.

Pain is just pain, but this hurt is growing desperate. I'm crying now through gritted teeth. My bloody handiwork blurs through the wet lens of my tears.

I need something to stop the blood. I shimmy out of overshirt and undershirt, back into overshirt. The soft undershirt I roll up tight against my bleeding scratched arm. I pull the cloth against the pain.

I pull it tight—and tighter still.

It helps.

Our clothes are not our own.

Each morning before breakfast, we queue as the Voice calls out our monikers and take our turns in dressing rooms. There are lots of dressing rooms but not so many as our bunks. I wait, patient with all rapt children until a dressing room comes free.

With fingertips, I open up the cubby as I do each meal to take my fodder tray. The cubby's empty, waiting for my dirty clothes. I take off all, except the bandage shirt, which comes slow, stiff with drying blood. Such ugly scabs. The shirt is stained. I wad up all ugliness, toss it inside, close the cubby shut.

After, the room cleans me. Mist comes from all spots at once. It's wet and dry, all the same time. It makes me fresh. But also stings so bad in my fresh cuts, I must chomp down on my other hand to keep from yelling out. It stinks like clean, and on my arm, it feels like a thousand needles new.

My cleanse all done, I check the cubby once again. Inside, there's all new clothes. Just like the ones I put inside but clean and mint condition. Don't smell like me. Or much at all.

I wonder, shower thoughts—are these the same pajamas, just cleaned? Like I am cleaned, and at the same time, too? Or does the cubby take the old, swallow it like breakfast, and just as quick produce the new?

It is a mystery.

These clothes shed no new light. The undershirt is lily-white, no sign nor smear of crusty blood. I wrap my arm as before. I put on the other clothes.

I'll do the same again.

This world makes all things from itself. It knows what we need and when and where and how to give. Somehow, our fingers speak to cubbies everywhere, and cubbies give us what we need. Then, take back when we're done.

But now, I own one thing. A syringe whose sharpness belongs only to me. That is what makes it sweet.

At breakfast, Gor asks me, "What's bad?" He sees my dark-shadowed eyes, my pain-stretched smile. He touches me on my lacerated limb, and I don't mean to, but I flinch to the feel.

He doesn't understand. I see his sadness. But he shrugs those feels away. We do this always; there is so much unknown. We cannot hold it. It is slipped and gone.

I'm Lolo. He's Gor. This much is true.

It's not enough.

"Eat this pudding," he says, pushing his cup toward me, his smile a question. This face I know.

"Thank you, Gor," I say. "Yummy." He watches, now smiling sure.

I eat. It's very sweet.

(tess)

{ HERE, WHERE CHILDREN PLAY. FLOOR IS SOFT, SITTING
cross-legged, sit in circle 'round some castle built from
blocks—take one block away, add one block. Blocks
stick together. Children build higher.

Holding marbles, squeezing tight. Marbles smooth
and polished, touch is safe, feels like home. Marble
is orange, flecked with red fire. Marble is blue and
turquoise like a planet to hold all life. Marble is violet.
Marble is yellow and gold, and marble stares with a
narrowed eye.

Holding hands behind back, touching marbles,
squeezing tight. Feel afraid.

Building the castle—take one block away, add one
block. Voice speaks from room. On the wall is a castle.
Seeing picture, listening to the Voice, building castle.

Marbles inside one hand, then inside the other.
Marble in mouth, held against cheek. Feel worried.

Marble tastes like . . . Tess. Does not go down throat.
Marble stays in mouth.

Tess. Tess spits out marble. Marble goes in hand.
Stomach hurts. Throat sore. Nose sniffles. Pain is fear,

and fear is pain, and Tess sits in room where children play. Tess does not play.

A girl cries. When children cry, Tess feels sad. Tess feels like crying too. Girl is not Tess, but Tess likes girl. Tess gets out from beanbag chair. Tess walks to girl. Girl sits against wall. Girl covers face with hands, makes snuffle noises.

Tess holds marbles in one hand. Tess touches girl with other hand. Girl looks up. Girl's face is wet. Stomach hurts more. Nose sniffles again.

"Why crying?" Tess says. Girl cries more. "Why crying?" Girl does not answer. Tess gives girl marble. Marble is violet. Girl takes marble. Tess rubs girl's hair. "Shh. Shh."

"Stomach hurts," girl says, and Tess understands. Tess wraps arm around girl. Tess gives marble. Girl squeezes marble. Tess squeezes marbles, too. Children fill this room and play.

"Tess," Tess says with hand to chest.

"Ree," girl says with hand to chest.

Together, we sit and watch the children play. Together, we squeeze marbles. Tess and Ree.

Now, we are two while children play. Children see the picture of the castle, and children listen to the Voice and children take blocks and add blocks.

We sit against the wall, and we watch. We are two.

My stomach hurts not as much. My throat not so sore. I'm Tess. I'm half of two.

The Caretakers walk in. The Caretakers look with black-pebble eyes. The Caretakers point at Ree. She cries.

Ree cried before and stopped, and now, she cries again. I remember.

I remember this: I was alone on the other side of the room, sitting in the beanbag chair, sitting with marbles.

Now, I am with the girl, and the girl is called Ree, and I am called Tess, and we are together.

In one hand, I am holding marbles, and with the other, I am holding hands with Ree. In one hand, Ree is holding marbles, and with the other, she holds mine. She is crying because the Caretakers want to take her, and she doesn't want to go.

They hold her shoulders. They pull her up. She drops the marbles. I am crying too. The Caretakers make all children feel worried, sad, afraid. The Caretakers smell like something bad. When the Caretakers walk into the room, bad things happen. The Caretakers never speak.

Ree is gone, and I sit against the wall, alone again. I have four marbles. I miss Ree. Everything hurts. I count my marbles. I still have four marbles. I am alone, Ree is gone. I just found her: we were two, I was half.

But now, alone again, just one. My throat hurts from tears. I feel I'll sleep from hurting loss.

The pulse comes—

A blinding flash, a screaming blare, a pain in every part, the world erased.

The pulse goes.

Here in room where children play. Soft floor. Hard wall. Marbles roll on floor. Holding marbles. Orange. Blue. Purple. Gold.

Building a castle while the Voice tells what to do.

Rubbing nose. Nose sniffles. Face wet. Wipes cheeks. Feeling sad.

Voice speaks a code. Standing. Code means stand, code means come, but only . . . Tess.

Code calls Tess, like the Caretakers, but without touch. Code draws her forward.

Tess doesn't decide. Tess obeys.

Tess knows what to do. Tess walks to door. She did not know this door before. In middle of door at Tess height, a half-circle of five hollows. Tess has five fingers. She presses five fingertips to five hollows.

The door is open.

Tess walks down hallway. Lights flash. She knows to follow the light.

What happens after lights? What happens after lights? *Tess can't remember. Tess doesn't know.*

Tess is afraid.

She doesn't want to walk. She doesn't want to move. The lights compel her. She follows the trail. Something bad happens now. She knows. She doesn't know. Her stomach hurts. Her throat hurts.

Tess is afraid.

The lights lead her to a room with the Caretakers. In the center of the room is a molded narrow cot. She's in a trance. She's numb. She lies on the cot.

They strap her down. Tess cannot move.

"What happens?" Tess asks the Caretakers.

They will not answer. They cannot speak.

I'm Tess. I *speak. "Why Tess? Why here? Does it hurt?"*

I ask them. They do not answer me.

The Caretakers cut away my shirt. My stomach is bare to bright lights, cool breeze. I watch. The Caretakers rub cold gel on my skin. I shiver. I want to cry but can't. I'm numb. My stomach, too. My side feels nothing.

I watch the scalpel. I watch the cut. They divide flesh from flesh and pull my self aside.

They reach inside. They rummage.

I don't feel a thing. I'm not afraid. The pain is fear, and fear is pain, and for now, the pain is gone and the fear is gone, too.

From my side, the Caretakers produce a clear sac, the size of my palm, filled with murky fluid. They transfer it to a container. They produce a large syringe, inject another murky fluid into the cavity within my side, and close the wound. They knit the edges together. They spray it whole.

On the cot, I feel some clarity. The fear becomes terror. The pain becomes nothing. The worry becomes panic. The dread becomes despair. The nightmare that slips away with every pulse, always a lurker, always a shadow: it is here. It can be touched. This is the horror. This is hell.

On the cot, I can think.

The Caretakers stand beside me one on either side. I'm paralyzed. A Caretaker produces another syringe, another needle, another murky fluid. It places the needle against my neck. The point pierces. I can't cry out. I feel the fluid pumping in, I feel it pulsing in veins.

Another pulse—

Shake, tremble, shiver, seize.

All done. All gone.

Lying on cot. Alone in room. Bright lights.

Lifting hand, seeing palm. Seeing symbols on each fingertip.

The symbols stand for . . . Tess.

Why this room? Why this cot?

Tess sits up. Tess slides bare feet onto the floor. Tess stands and totters; feels sick and woozy. She wants to throw up. She cannot walk. She waits for legs to work again. The Voice speaks. The lights flash. Tess follows.

She's in the room where children play.

Girl sits beside. Girl touches arm. Girl gives Tess marble. Tess looks at marble. Orange flecked with red. She puts the marble in her mouth. Girl strokes her hair. This part is good.

}

(lolo)

THERE COMES A NIGHT I CANNOT WRITE. MY TIREDNESS SLURPS ALL through my bones—I feel it hard in every thought.

So weary from questions: facts I can't recollect, days I can't recall. My skin is filled with scars, some fresh, some scabbed. I'm losing space to cut. I hurt all times and every day. I hurt inside my chest.

I hurt with a rust-red crisscross labyrinth of the wounds across my legs, my arms, my side.

I hurt inside my heart.

This night, I'm swaddled in my bunk. There sounds the *beep-booping* of machines, the breathing of rapt children. The structure breathes, too, exhaling air, inhaling back. These unquiet rustlings, these songful hums.

I tell myself, *Be strong.* I tell myself, *Be brave.*

I am Lolo, and I am the child that remembered writing. I am the one that could save us all. I can't grow tired. I can't be afraid. Pain is just pain.

But this night, I can't steel myself against the cuts.

"Gor?" I say.

"Lolo?"

"Can I come down?"

"Yes."

I drop myself down this stable ladder, wincing against the pain in arms and legs, resisting urges that my groans and whimpers show. Gor cannot hear; Gor cannot know.

I crawl into his Gor-stink sheets. He wraps his arm around my shoulder. He brushes my forearm's wound. It hurts me, but I don't cry out.

"How do you feel?" Gor asks me. I do not remember a time before when Gor spoke these words. I didn't know he knew such things. He must have learned in his own memory-duties what these complicated words mean.

"Tired," I say. "I feel tired."

"I feel tired," Gor says. "I want to go home."

His speech brings up such thick and awful feelings. It comes unexpected, so I can't hold back. My throat is sore, my eyes brimming with hot tears. I feel a lurch inside my chest. I know that feeling. Such few words hold all this feel.

"Go home," I repeat. I shape the words myself. This speech transforms me everywhere. This want becomes my heart.

The feels are everything, but I don't know what they mean.

It's been long since I lay tight in this bunk with Gor. Some days, some nights. I don't know numbers. This absence is distance, getting wider. This lack is the empty feeling in my arms, but I wriggle my front to his back, hold dear. It's been long. Does he know?

I don't know what he knows. Our time is shot with holes.

I think of the Caretakers: it's different for them. What one knows, all know. Their thoughts are not their own. What one sees, all see. The Voice speaks to them in ways we cannot hear. For children, the Voice is sound. For Caretakers, the Voice is something else. They have no secrets. They have no gaps. They live like one being in many parts.

What comfort, I think. If we could be like them. If we never had to feel alone again. If Gor and I were not two but one. And I knew his memories and thoughts. And he knew mine. And children would not recount their dreams because the dream would hold us all.

If we felt no need to hold our stories because they were held somewhere else. No spaces between us. No walls to separate.

This thought comes to me: one day we will be like the Caretakers. The Voice will speak in silence, and we will hear. I will be Gor, and Gor will be me. The structure will know us all. The story will be shared.

I squeeze tight against Gor's bony shoulders, against these *mournesome* thoughts. In this now, our bodies hold us: my blood-marked flesh is vast and wide, my thoughts beyond a gulf that can't be crossed. Gor squeezes my hand, draped against his own soft belly. I feel his breathing; he feels mine. There is no prick of needle nor gold syringe, but still, I feel the bliss wash over me, the lapping of the light. Gor smells like home.

"I know about before," he says.

"Before what?"

"Before now."

I wait in silent mirth, laughing quiet in my chest, lest he say again breakfast. But he doesn't speak.

"What was before?" I ask finally.

"Home," he says. "Home was before."

Again, that feeling, like I'm struck. For a moment, I can't breathe. The love and longing, the need and loss, all rising up. That feel like tubing in my throat.

"We'll go," I say. "We'll go, Gor."

This now is here. I'm Lolo. He's Gor. Together in this bubble as we've been before. This night, we sleep soft in tangle of warm limbs and samelike smell of breath and farts.

In this now, there is a slope of grassy hillside. Green grass tickles rough and tender on bare legs, leaving woven mesh patterns against my skin. Undeterred, I lay content in emerald stubble, disregarding such prickles, such tickles, such itching delight. Burrowing fingertips into dirt, feeling earth embrace the whorls.

The world smells mouth-watering scrumptious. Dad tends the grill, the fire flickers with the lip-smacking savory of sizzling meats. Mom on the deck, arranging mustard and ketchup, setting out plates.

I stare up at endless sky falling toward the hush of periwinkle. The first star is Venus; the first star is another world.

The first stars twinkle splendorous against the fading light while bats swoop and dive, wheeling like fighter planes, mosquitoes their prey. The cicadas carry the song of a whir and drone and purr so loud it drowns.

Upon me flops this golden *fursome* beast, rough tongue aflap, wet jowls adrip, black nose all cold and snuffle. He pants and lolls and licks, and I groan and laugh beneath the doting weight.

Beside me, some giggles: just near my shoulder is Tess, sitting prim on a blanket with knees pulled up and sparkle-polished toes. "Ugh! Bentley, off," I grumble and huff from my mutt-flattened chest.

And he's off, my thighs the launch pad to run and pant another lap.

Tess sits statue-still with perfect gaze. Tess watches the world. Tess longs to catch a firefly, so she waits and wills the flickering aviators to come to her. I tell her I can catch one faster. She dares me. I bet her. But while she persists in her patient pose, I flail and grab at golden cosmonauts. Each wandering lightning bug escapes my grasp.

Meanwhile, Bentley has set his sights to catch a hot dog. He lingers in usual fashion around the grill, evincing innocence. "Get lost, Bentley," Dad says and tests a beefy patty. This dog is naught but wounded dignity and sits paws forward, wholly courteous. His manner suggests he is only here to help. Dad deposits a half-dozen charred franks upon the plate and turns back to the grill.

Bentley!

He's up like a shot, grabs one frank between his jaws, races hasty. A great hue and cry goes up from the man behind the grill. Dad chases the dog across the yard, waving his grease-charred spatula all the way while the dog gobbles it all in one choking gulp, greedy as can be. Dad yells. Bentley licks his chops, not even pretending regret. Tess and I laugh until our sides hurt, and we almost can't contain our pee.

Bentley slinks away to nurse his paws and gloat. The rest of us take our greedy selves to the deck and fill our plates to feast on picnic fare.

Night falls. Darkness comes. The sky is star-spangled indigo. We settle upon the blanket, Tess and I beside—Bentley between us, snoring now, our fingers buried in his golden scruff.

We are like this when the first fireworks flare and spark across the sky, emerging from beyond the trees, like rage confetti being born. Bentley is alarmed by such pyrotechnics. With the second outburst, he rears up like a startled horse and whines and scratches at our hands, determined to alert us to these perils.

"Shh, Bentley," we say.

"Put him inside," Dad says, still tending grievance for the hot dog incident.

"But he'll be scared," Tess says when luminescence bursts with splitting thunderclaps once more. Bentley is quite unamused. He cowers, trembles. "I'll go with him," Tess volunteers, and something inside me stirs. My sister should not miss this rocket show we cherish. Such magics only happen once a year.

But Bentley quivers pitiful, clearly caught between two yearnings: the urge to run far and fast and the need to bury his trembling snout between our knees for harbor. And Tess is concerned only for this sad creature, earnest to bring him somewhere safe.

In that firecracker-dazzled instant, I see my sister unobscured, her distinct and unrepeated self. This amorphous person who has been beside me all my life sharpens into focus as a rare and peerless soul. Her innermost life unknown to me yet still a matter of fact. By this revelation, I'm stunned (as more explosions sparkle).

"I'll go, too," I say.

And this decides eternity. Our paths are fixed. Our destiny resolved. There is no turning back from everything to come. There is no end to how long the infinite can be. Together, with blinds closed against the racket and tumult, my sister and I cuddle and *snarfle* our fear-farting dog upon the couch until the pyrotechnics pass.

In my bunk at night, I make my sharp ink. I draw a dog. I draw a girl. I draw a lightning bug aflame. I draw explosions in the sky. I draw another girl.

These visions of a home are built on senses I've forgotten. The scent of grass. The smell of meat. The taste of ketchup. The feel of bare feet upon the frazzled ground. The breeze in my hair. The furry beast.

I remember the feeling of remembering. I remember thoughts about the thing.

Though I can't recall the thing itself.

Infused with yearning, I try to draw these sensations I've forgotten. I hold them to myself like magic spells. I build them from broken building blocks.

I get angry with myself. It hurts so much to render these stupid symbols on this wall, and they barely even brush the truth. They are so far from the feeling they seek to hold.

My tentative scrawlings are like me: a search for words I cannot know, to ask the questions I still can't form, for answers I do not and may never vision.

Reaching, grasping, blindfolded, and bound.

Not even close to close enough.

Gor and I file into the breakfast hall, surrounded on all sides by children. On the surface, all seems the same: bright lights, long tables. The walls glow yellow, their often morning hue. We line up one by one to press our fingertips to the space above each cubby and reveal our breakfast trays. The Caretakers offer their dead dull gaze. Chatter ebbs and flows as we try our voices again.

On the surface, all seems the same, but underneath, something's changed. As I wait, I puzzle out this different feeling, handle its aspects in my mind.

Same acid glare. Same chow drowned in awful brown. Same cold and leathered meats. Same lackluster pajamas.

I press my fingertips. I take my tray.

As I walk back to my customary spot, I see it: we've become tight-knotted camps. The children sit in clusters. Each closed in a circle to themselves, their conversation eager yet quiet as if they hope the others do not hear.

Around Gor and I, the sitting's sparse. It seems we are left this skimpy handful of children with no clique.

Gor is undisturbed. He scarfs down heaped forkfuls of some gloppy eats. I sit beside. I perk my ears and strain for fragments of the others' talk.

It is, as always, talk of visions and memories and muffled dreams.

I pat Gor's forearm. "Stay. I'll be back." He nods, mouth full. I grab my tray and sidle over to the closest bunch of conspiring children. They scooch to welcome me into their company and wait, expectant for my story.

But I am canny. I hold my cards. Instead, I press them with one question I've come to know must matter most: "How do you remember home?"

Eyes alight, they tell me of their towering world. This needle pierced from ground to sky, and them in the middle, suspended somewhere miles above the brown ground flecked with silver, the brown sky streaked with cream. How they scampered and ran in its tunnels and shafts and played amongst the humming tanks where food grew and fuel brewed. And took the elevator as far up as they dared, always climbing further toward the sky—never quite reaching. But they dreamed they'd reach the top. The ground was *yesterday*. The sky *tomorrow*. These time-meaning words they toss with certainty.

"How did it end?" I ask.

But this they cannot say. And they eye me with suspicion. Suspecting now that I am not with them, that their past is not my own. Our fragile stories cannot bear opposition. And indeed, I know this odd tale they've constructed—a tower vaster than any city—'tis but a dream. There's no such edifice. There's no such place. They are much mistaken.

But I will not disabuse rapt children of their notions. Regretful, I take my tray and move on to the next.

These kids claim to hail from a world called Moon, their home a shimmering bubble on a plane of polished rock. Above, the searing night, the diamond stars, the stretching on eternal. How quiet it must be, that dusty moonscape, undisturbed by human footstep. The kind of world where a labyrinth like our own might thrive. But they describe it lovingly.

"How did it end?"

This they know. I see it in their eyes, their heart-numb gaze, their trembling lips. The bubble pierced. The high-pitched roar as their breathings leaked away. The roar of machinery, the clang of sirens, every warning signal at once to warn at panicked volumes, to let loose bellows and wails. And this, better than silence. Silence is the worst.

They grow sober as they speak of how it feels when air runs out, the fluttering in their chests, the weak overwhelm, lips blue, blacking out. Then seeing the slick, dark orbs of the Caretakers, peering close—too close—inspecting swollen, lifeless tongues.

They are delusional, too. So I leave behind their huddle.

Other children tell of tents strung up in canopies of green. They pranced on swaying catwalks, stretched from tree to tallest tree. They dropped leaves onto the breathing, screeching green beneath. The constant chatter of birds and sweet glimmer of the dew.

But then—I'm rattled to see the girl crying as she tries to speak—the whole ground shakes, like earthquakes, as ancient trees bigger 'round than all this room are ripped and tossed like twigs. When they fall, the whole earth trembles. The forestworld turns topsy-turvy as the Harvesters destroy it all. The birds shriek in panicked fright. The sky rains blood and feathers.

I'm discouraged by their stupid thoughts. I come back around to Gor.

As I made my tours of these raving bands of lunatics around the lengthy table, Gor struck up conversation with those nearest us, or they with him. Timid but jubilant, they cite the allure of the ice cream truck, the patter of flip-flops, the feeling of sand between their toes. They remember a snowman in winter with a carrot for a nose, the mug of cocoa with melting cream, the sting of chapped and bloody lips, the fire's bright blaze.

Such nows I have not felt myself, yet at some core level, I feel their truth. I don't know how I know. This sense of coming home, it simply fills my bones.

With tear-choked throat, I share what memories I can.

In this now, a looming space with herds of frightened children, ragged breath and staring eyes, moving across the concrete floor. Shivering and much afraid.

Overhead, the roof is almost too far removed to see, where darkness gathers among the metal rafters.

We huddle close, one to another against the cold and windy drafts. It comes to me: this warehouse is larger than an airplane hangar. There are enough children in this place to populate another world.

And I am with my sister, Tess. We are together as we've been now all along. I hold her hand tight as can be. I am still the youngest, though only slightly smaller. I need her badly, as she needs me. We cling to each other and wait to see what days or times will come. And though my heart is beating hard and fast and my breath is coming quick, though my throat is hard and tight and shivers rattle through my trembling frame, I know we are together. This we have, at least.

I have forgotten all befores. Already, I cannot remember how we came to be inside this massive loft nor what happened to allow this circumstance. I recognize no faces among the crying, bleating children.

The Caretakers emerge into the room from some door we cannot see. So many, more than we've ever seen before, all congregated in one place. They stream in all directions like a horde of insects, like a nest of ants disturbed.

Tess and I cling still tighter, determined that we should not be separated. They will not pry our hands apart.

As the Caretakers approach, they bring overwhelming dread with them like a nightmare, a gross and creeping cloud. They make the edges of my sight feel dim and dark and fogged. My stomach churns, and all this story swirls along the edges. A rushing in my ears. A conviction that the world must end.

The Caretakers grip some kind of tool and press it to the forehead of each child. It whirs and grinds and emits a glare of light. With beeps and whistles, this scanner tells them something.

Tess and I watch all this with trepidation.

Until the Caretakers come to us. They scan her head, then mine, with a tickling, prickling presence just past the edges of my brain. It's like a shadow creeping close. It doesn't hurt. But it makes my stomach flip-flop, feel strange.

They point their pale and clammy fingers at our entwined sister hands. They do not speak. They can't. Nonetheless, we grasp their point: let go our fingers. We refuse.

The two of them with damp and bony hands grip fast the two of us. They clamp our hands. They are stronger than they look: limp and moist but forceful. They pry apart our fingers, and though we shriek and flail, there's little we can do. We are separated. We are two.

Grabbing fast to my right hand so tight it hurts, the Caretaker splays apart my fingers. He holds my palm to the scanning tool's hot edge. Fast as lighting, it imprints a symbol on each fingertip. My hand stings, but it's all too quick to badly hurt.

Soon as this code is imprinted, the Caretaker releases me. It lets go, and I almost fall. I gaze with wonder at my palm, the symbol etched upon each whorl. This blackly purple ink, suspended just beneath the skin as if always part of me.

I look for Tess, to show her, to see if they've done the same to her. I look for her, to take her hand in mine.

But she's gone. In mounting panic, I scan the room. I see only lost and frightened children, so many sobbing faces.

I glimpse her back, her hair. They're pulling her away. She's peering over her right shoulder and trying to fight back. But the Caretakers drag her forward.

I lose sight of her amongst all the other roiling kids.

I take off in a run. I swerve and dodge, not bothering to say, *Excuse me*, tripping and falling more than once but pushing on. With force of sorrow, I will this crowd to part for me.

Once past this wave of children, I reach these towering glass cubes. Four walls, one roof, perfectly encased, this massive cage all made of glass.

There are six—seven—ten—twelve—too many to count. Each fills up with children as the Caretakers sort all kids into these vast transparent hulls.

I see in time, just soon enough, as Tess is herded in this glass. The crate is filled with children, all teeming, frightened, stampeding. I run as fast as I can, tripping over all and sundry, to get into this same box.

Before I'm there, the door slides shut. The edges seal.

This glass is now impermeable, as if those doors were never there at all.

I run around all sides, panting, frantic, heaving, searching for an opening. Instead, I see my sister, looking sadly through the glass. I stand on one side; she on the other.

I slap the glass with *mournesome* sobs and rage that I can't break through. She does not rage. It's not her way. She's still and quiet as a marble statue.

She places her palm flat against the glass. On the tips of her fingers, I see her own black-purple code. Five symbols.

These letters or numbers or icons—whatever they are, these ideograms—they are emblazoned deep and pure upon my brain. This stark and graven image remains when nothing else remains. This awful vision I will not ever shake.

There's a sort of grinding, a sound like—a steel ship hull run aground into a granite cliff? A grating sound like this. The floor opens up, becomes a tunnel or a well or a massive shaft into a cave. Her glass box drops, descends, is sucked away. And with it Tess.

But now I know: the tattoo etched into her fingertips is inscribed inside my heart. I don't know what the symbols mean. But I know how they look.

This piece I can record. This knowledge I can keep.

I paint this code upon the wall above my bunk. I make it my study.

I learn this code as if it were my own.

The children in the memory lab, we do not leave. We have our sleeping bunks inside our pods, our room for meals, our dressing hall where cleaning happens. We have our parlor where some children talk and others play, and always, there are mystic puzzles, strange games, shifting heaps of blocks that join each other when they touch, becoming different shapes. The Caretakers prod us to the parlor, and the Voice speaks that we play, and we obey—to disobey brings pain. We go to the pedal room for exercise.

Of course, we have the fearsome spaces with chairs that bind and the

Caretakers watching in each corner. In these rooms, we remember all nows that came before. And also, we forget.

There are other halls with other labs and other rooms, all filled with tools that make us tremble, shiver, weep. These, too, we can visit if we wish. All are marked with one large symbol glimmering on the walls.

Beyond, we do not go.

It's wrong to walk in passages marked with other emblems. Why, I cannot say. I don't recall what teachings made us know. If pressed, I could supply no reasons why the symbol looming in this concourse must be our whole entire world.

But walking in the light of other symbols is like neglecting the order of the Voice. It makes the body ache. It grips the chest with cold. It makes my fingers itch and makes my stomach churn, like heaving silver schools of fish (I know I've seen on tranquil screens). With every step, the pain comes worse, and I am more compelled to run.

In visions, I've seen the structure climb. I've seen this labyrinth built in the wreckage of our worldly home (sweet place of flitting fireflies and grass as green as our dwelling's walls at lunchtime). I know how vast the maze must be. And yet, we stay in this tight space. Confined to the narrow by our own capricious feels.

Some moments I know: my sister is here. Somewhere in this tangled maze, she is. I don't know how to get to her. Not yet. But I will.

This I know: I will.

It comes to me.

There are whole hours, perhaps whole days, when I forget this code carved on my fingertips. It is with me like breathing. It calls me hither and yon; it summons me to take my lunch tray in my turn, to bring myself to memory rooms like a pirate walks a plank. These things I do without quite knowing. Sleepwalking, here and there.

Then, sometimes, I turn my palm and gaze in wonderment at these characters.

One breakfast, I cup my palm and look. It's there, of course. There all along. My breath catches quick.

I see it for what it is: my own monogram. Written on my body, which must hold all of me, all that I feel and know, however little this might be. This code my own.

And in this moment, I notice—for the first time? Nothing here is for the first time, that I'm sure—I notice the first symbol, etched into my thumb, is the same that hovers on the wall of every space in our rapt children's lair.

I look to that hologram and back to my first stubby finger.

Hasty and ill-mannered, I grab Gor's hand, knocking his flimsy fork away. (Ever good-natured, Gor does not reproach, just scoops his morsels with his other hand, eating lumps with fingers bare.) I turn his palm upward, compare his tattoo to my own. His thumb's the same. This symbol, we share.

My thoughts grow quick. I run from kid to kid, grabbing hands, comparing. I do not tell them what I think. This secret is my own.

We share the same mark on our thumbs. It marks our territory, what places we can travel without rousing thoughts of buried traumas.

This now, I know. I know this map, the map that leads to her.

Before I leave, I bow beside the breakfast table and palm that fallen fork. I slip it up my sleeve. I do not need this fork. It has no urgent attributes nor skills. But I know now what it is to own something, to save one small token for myself. The feel is sweet.

I sneak back to my bunk. I pull back my mat to reveal the secret stash: things I've nabbed to be all my own. Syringe, first. My own first property. Then other bits and bobs: some strips of cloth from undershirts. A stolen block. A purloined spoon. A pilfered sweet, now surely stale.

My fork now joins the hoard.

Stretched out flat, I study the code etched in flaking rust upon the wall.

This is all I have. This is all I know.

Somehow, it must guide me.

At night, I wait to hear Gor's steady snores below. I lay silent, eyes open, back flat and arms straight. I gaze up at my bubble's curve and imagine I can see the before-world. When there were lawns and dogs and bikes and stars.

'Til Gor's snuffling breaths come thick and heavy. My time is now.

I slip from bed. I tread soft upon the rails, down the ladder, past my slumbering Gor. Then tiptoe down this lengthy hallway where pods and pods stretch out for lonesome miles, rapt children fast asleep inside each one. The machine lights flicker on the walls. The glimmering arrows point to other prisons. The floor in these halls is always springy-soft, like molded bunks, so there's not much need to tiptoe. I do it, still.

I hold my breath as children stir and murmur, as sheets rustle and breathing shifts. They are lost in dreams. They pay me no mind.

I see a clump of the Caretakers at the junction where the arrows turn to other halls. I gasp, afraid of what will happen if I'm caught: something bad, I know. I can't remember what but feel such things will not end well.

I flatten myself against the wall as small and shadowlike as I can. And wait.

Their pale bald heads are turned away from me, so no eyes watch. I flit on past.

Into some vestibule. The door closes, and I'm in an empty room. Nothing but floors and walls, like someone commenced to build and forgot to finish. The floor glows softly, and in this dim luminescence, I see no other door.

But there are facts I know about this place: not all doors are easily seen. Some are hidden, wearing odd camouflage for reasons of their own. Some doors occur where there was no door before. Some doors are made through force of will.

I start from where I am. Pacing slow along the wall, my gentle fingers searching. Reaching high, reaching low. Exploring with my hands.

I reach a corner. I start afresh.

I go on in this fashion until my fingertips find a place they fit, five muted circles too tentative to see. I rest them there until I feel that tingling pulse. My whorls, that wall: they interface. I give command.

There is the door. I go on through.

The hard part starts.

A novel symbol hovers on these walls. Like two squiggle lines married by a slash. This symbol is not imprinted on my thumb, nor my sister's. This place is just a place that separates. So I walk on through. But the pains begin.

It starts in my chest, this panicked feeling. This tightness, like I cannot breathe. I feel like crying out, begging for air, but I know I must not make a peep.

My stomach roils, all insides shrinking inward, clenching like a fist.

It's like pain but also like pain's dread.

Like something stalking me, a dread horde just beyond my shoulder but always drawing nearer.

(A Harvester, ripping children's limbs, spraying, squirting, barfing blood.)

A coffin that encloses, buried beneath the miles of earth, the ground pressing always closer still.

(A wave of blood.)

Something that will surely hurt or kill me soon, my stubborn self as fragile as a robin's egg.

I walk. I drag my feet along, no matter how they wish to slow. I force myself to pace through all the stomach heaves and heart tremors. I tell myself it's not so bad.

It isn't, though my tears come fast now, trudging down this endless hall, and my jaw aches from clenching.

I do it still.

For a moment, I think to give up, retreat. I turn around. Fall back a step or two. Away from here and back to home. And with this sudden swerve, all my body's warning signs desist. I feel flooding relief.

But I don't surrender. I have to find my sister before I forget again. I will forget. We all forget. Time is *short*.

Another word for time is short.

So I turn my face toward the future, toward the space ahead that hurts, and resolute through all that dread and angst, I go.

I am Lolo, the child who remembered writing, the child who gave her blood, the girl who remembered true the world as it was. And this pain is not too much.

But as I press on, I flash on momentary thoughts of tortures. Of being prodded through these forbidden hallways by the Caretakers wielding pointed sticks. We step, are shocked. Fall back screaming, are poked again, step forward, are shocked again. Again, again.

I will not let this vision surface. I press it down, fierce and forceful as I can. That now is past. This pain is only echoes.

I come to a new symbol: a circle within, a circle without. I see no Caretakers. This is some unending tunnel that connects many others, maybe all. These tunnel walls are dark like charcoal and blank without markings. No lighted arrows show the way. The floor's firm and unyielding, not like the springy softness where rapt children tread.

I keep on going.

I come to a crossroads. I don't know how to choose between two ways. One to my one hand, one to my other. I stare at my fingertips as if they hold the answer. I search my tremors.

I search my mind, but I can't tell if I've been at this spot never, once, or a million times before. There is always this sense: all of this has happened before, all of this will happen again. But I'm certain on no moment but the present.

This now is all.

Unknowing if it's memory or whim, I choose left.

And walk and walk. And take more turns. Until I know I'm lost for sure.

Those pains have quieted, but I'm sore all over. My body aches from holding back, from suffocating all I feel. I feel such hurt. I'm tired.

I thought I could find her: such silliness and such delusions. I am no better than the raving children with their tales of endless skyscrapers and bubbles on the moon and swinging ropes that link the ancient trees. I, too, tell myself stories that can't be true. To live in this nightmare without a story would be too much to bear.

I sit down for a while, rub my hurting feet. I pick at blisters and worry at my aching toes. For the longest time—truth be told, I can't remember quite how long—my world has been no bigger than an acorn. My body struggles with such distances.

Perhaps, this night I walked halfway across the world.

Tired, I drift briefly to sleep, sitting there against the polished emptiness of a hard black wall.

In a dream, my long-lost Bentley nudges me. His cold wet snout touches my own small nose. He puts his scruffy paw in mine. "Get up," he woofs. "Get up."

I open my eyes. No golden beast to love. But still I stand.

I drag myself forward. The light is ramping up, the glow inside the walls slowly growing bright.

Just ahead, I see what I seek: a triangle, inside a square.

It is a jolt. This vision I'd been holding close, now so large and real. The symbol I inscribed upon the wall, remembered from my sister's thumb in dreams. Now here.

And something else. I remember. *I remember*—I can't say what.

But pain stabs across my side, and for a moment, I catch my breath, grab hard myself. It passes.

This pain is echoes too.

I search for the door into this next place.

(tess)

Here in morning room, waiting for breakfast. Sitting at long table, all in rows. Walk to cubbies. Take each tray.

No breakfast yet. Sitting. Waiting. Patient, too.

Tess. Tess is patient.

Tess holds two marbles. Marbles smooth and polished, touch is safe, feels like home. Marble is yellow. Marble is violet.

Girl sits by Tess. Girl looks different. Not like other children. Tess wears blue. All children wear blue. Girl wears white. Girl's hair is rough, short-shorn stubble.

Girl takes Tess's hand. Not marble hand. Other hand. Tess gives hand without fighting. Girl seems nice. Tess feels afraid.

Tess always feels afraid. But she's not afraid of the girl.

Girl looks at Tess's hand, touches each finger. Tess looks, too. Tess sees the squiggles on each tip. Tess doesn't know what squiggles mean. But the girl seems happy. Wraps arms around Tess, and Tess feels happy too.

I'm Tess. And feeling happy, too.

Girl shakes my hand, shows me her fingers, shows me my fingers. She's talking lots and loud. "Sister," the girl says. "My sister. I found you now. Do you remember me?"

I smile but feel confused. I don't mind sitting next to the girl. I like her face. I like her dark eyes, her fuzzy head.

"What about Bentley-dog?" the girl says. "Do you remember him? Do you remember ice cream? Do you remember crunching through fallen leaves?"

I shrug. Don't know. Girl is happy but so sad, too. What does it mean?

The girl keeps talking. "I remembered you."

I remember remembering.

"From other nows," the girl says.

I remember such a thing as other nows could be.

"I saw in dreams," the girl says.

I can almost remember what it feels to dream.

"Did you remember me? Did you see me too?"

I shrug. No. Girl is getting loud. Some children look. Most don't. These children here do not much wonder.

Girl is sad. All sad now.

I don't know why, but I am feeling sad, too. And this sadness, like all my sad and sorry days, is because of what I feel but do not know.

I put my arm around her shoulder.

"I'm Lolo," she says. "Lolo." She wants me to remember. I tell myself this thing I will, just this thing alone. I put my marbles on the table. I never let them go. But just this once, I do.

I pull her head to me. With one arm 'round such bony shoulders. With one hand petting this girl's soft-stubble head. "Lolo," I say. "Okay. Okay."

Lolo cries. I don't know why.

She sits up, wiping snot. She looks at me. "What do they do to you?"

"Do? To me?" I know what she means to ask. I want to answer. I want to know myself. I cannot find the words.

"Here. What do they do to all these children here?"

I shrug again. I am Tess. I am here.

Lolo is here. Us two, together. This is all I know.

"Where does it hurt?"

I know this, too. I pull up blue scrub shirt and point to hurting side. This pain-knot lives always just there. First thing I know. Each thought I grasp. This pain.

Lolo moves her fingers gentle on the sore spot. I look as she looks. I see no scar. I thought to see a scar. "I'm sorry," *she says.*

"Did you hurt me there?" *I ask.*

"No," *Lolo says.* "Not me. Them." *She points across the room.*

I don't know them, and then, I do. The Caretakers. Tall in dark robes. Pale empty faces. No mouths. Can't speak. Black marble eyes. They're always here. I forgot these ghouls. But now I know. That pain. That fear. It's them.

I want to scream. This feel is too horrible to know. That we belong to them. That we do as they will. That they hurt us always and always still. And we're trapped like rats. I want to cry. To pound my fists upon this table. I want to call out to all rapt children, This world is hell. Let's run.

I feel it building. Expectant. Waiting. Dread. My hairs all tingle. My skin gets sharp. It's coming.

The pulse comes—

Gone. All.

The pulse goes.

Sitting at breakfast. No tray before. Waiting for food.

Girl beside. Girl waiting, watching.

Girl seems mad or something.

"Tess?" the girl says.

Tess. *Tess looks at girl. Why sit so close? Why wear white pajamas, not like Tess's blue?*

"Tess?" the girl says again. "You know me? Lolo? What happened just now? All rapt children sudden still?"

Tess doesn't say.

"Tell me," the girl says. "Where does it hurt?"

This, Tess knows. She feels it now. Tess points silent to her side.

"Me too," the girl says. "I hurt there too." Girl touches same side.

Tess feels sad. She doesn't know why. She can't remember. Chest hurts. Heart hurts. Throat hurts. She doesn't want that girl to hurt.

Tess looks for marbles. Marbles in hands or sometimes mouth. No marbles in hand. No marbles in mouth. But marbles on table. Marble is yellow. Marble is violet.

Marble makes Tess feel better. Tess—me. Marble makes me feel better. Marble feels like home.

I hold yellow marble. I give violet marble to girl. I don't want her to hurt.

Girl takes violet marble, clenched in fingers. She squeezes marble. I squeeze my marble too. I reach out and touch her stubbly head.

"Thank you," the girl says. "Next time. I promise. I'll find you in Paris."

Voice calls my number. Time for breakfast. I stand. I go to where it calls. I press five fingertips. I take my tray.

When I return with breakfast, girl is gone.

The pulse comes—

}

(1o1o)

I COMMENCE AGAIN MY JOURNEY HOME. THIS PART I DID NOT VISION; THIS trip I did not plan. I trudge along with heart like lead and cheeks all gross with tears. Not caring if I reach my place—except for Gor. My own Gor. At least, he knows me still.

This is what it is: no past, no future. All words for time are gone. So I did not think, what will happen next. I only moved. I saw my sister. She did not know me. What now? This now is now. I'm perplexed and bereft. And also lost. While my feet feel like two sodden strips of meat.

Come about, as I drag my travel-worn feet down some unfamiliar hallway. All alone—or so I think—I have cause to jump half-out my skin.

The Voice speaks. "Where are you going, rapt child Lolo?"

I answer cuz I must; there is no other way. "Not sure I exactly know, just now."

"Did you accomplish what you hoped?" the Voice inquires. Always persistent, pesky too. This Voice could question on for all of time. "Did you find out what you wished to know?"

I answer, of course, detached and weary. But what I feel is all despair. How foolish that I imagined I had slipped away unseen. I have never once been free. I have always been observed. There is no hope at all.

"Go left," the Voice tells me. I obey. Perhaps, it guides me home. Perhaps, I'm being sent to places unknown, prepped to begin all this insanity again.

I know now there is nothing I can do. I am some pawn.

Always I answer when the Voice speaks. But for the first time, alone in this unending labyrinth with naught but the Voice, no Caretakers to terrorize with their pale dread presence, it occurs to me that I could question the Voice.

"Why am I here?" I ask.

"Why not you? Why not us?" the Voice asks back. Can it only question?

"Where is home? What was before? Why did the Caretakers destroy the world?"

The Voice is silent for some time.

Perhaps, it's only I who is compelled to speak. The only needful answers are my own.

But then the Voice says, "There are things we would rewrite all of history to forget. Rapt child Lolo, be glad you do not know. That way, now. To the right."

"What are you?" I ask the Voice. "Why can't we see you?"

"You see me now," the Voice says. "I am this. This structure. I am them. The Caretakers. I am you, even."

"Why don't you have a name?"

"I am all of it. I don't need a name. I am we. I am us."

"But what *are you*, really?" We have changed places. Me, the questioner. And this thought fills me with exhilaration but also so much fear.

"I am the one who remembers, if you will. Try that hallway. You'll see a part of us that's not yet built. I am a work in progress. So are we all."

I go the way it tells. A sharp turn down the right. But it seems, as I walk along, this hallway is only growing longer. That it expands as I proceed. So I walk on.

Then, I see it up ahead: the passage ends. What lies beyond is not a wall but a window. An open space like a wound in this world. Through that opening, I see the sky.

A square of dark sky—this dark sky dotted with flaming stars.

The world outside. The world beyond. The world before.

I will stand on the edge of that precipice and see the city below. I'm sure of it. I'll gaze on the place that Gor and I once knew as our home. I'll find our way. So I must . . .

I fall to running, almost stumbling, and rush and race fast as I can toward that open space. It's like a dream. I run as fast I can but never fast enough.

I cannot close the gap.

The nanites swarm in from holes unseen. Perhaps, they come from outside the gap. A maddening cloud, they swarm and whir and coalesce. They converge. They knit the gap. They close the hole. They make it whole.

And I can't run fast enough.

When I reach the place, it's solid wall.

I scream with all my rage and sorrow. I pound this wall until my bruised knuckles split and bleed. There's nothing but the heat of fresh-built world-fabric and the lingering ozone stink.

The world is gone and all been taken.

The Voice waits for me to stop crying, and in soothing tones, it guides me directly to my laboratory home. Somewhere along the way, I think, *There was one hole, and now, it's gone. But there could be other holes.*

By the point I reach my home, brave and bold again. I am Lolo, don't forget. I will not give up. I think about the windows and the doors, the glimpses to the world outside.

I'm not afraid. I'm only fierce to find such other gaps.

First thing I do is search for Gor. I find him in the workshop, working at some puzzle I do not apprehend, shuffling back and forth these solid pieces in his solid hands. I grasp him hard, toss puzzle all away, grab and drag him to some corner.

My breath comes fast, my words tumble and sputter and traffic jam. I must tell him all. This I know.

He gazes blank and baffled at my frantic screechings as I beseech him, "Listen."

Listen. I escaped. I found a way. I found my sister. I found a hall. I found a hole.

There is something outside. And maybe home.

He thinks slow, this Gor. He is always good but not so bright. "You left here? You went to some other lab?"

Yes. Yes. I did it once. I can do it again. I slipped away, and no one saw, and no one stopped.

But that's not what matters most: the outside world is closer than we think. There is something out there, and it shimmers like our one-time home.

"Your sister. Your sister? Your sister."

I remember in my fist, clutched close, this purple marble my sister gave. I present my palm to Gor, uncurl fingers, show this polished violet orb. "She didn't know me. But she gave me this."

"Do I have a sister?" Gor asks, and this—this, I do not know.

"If not, then you can share my own," I tell him, generous; I dream of home. I am unselfish. I would not stoop to hoard our love.

"Share? When?"

When we go outside, Gor. When we escape. When we take with us Tess. When we find our way home. We can do it. This now, I know.

"Your hand," Gor says. "Who hurt your hand? Who hurt you, Lolo?"

"I hurt myself," I say and confess with some chagrin how I beat the wall in punishment for its lost aperture.

"But if there was one door. There could be more," Gor says.

Grudging, I must say he's right. Perhaps, he's quicker than I thought.

I'm forming words to tell him of the Voice and the mysteries it spoke. This I must tell him also, the Voice that remembers, the Voice that knows. That we live and breathe the body of the Voice. That somehow, somewhy, the Voice wanted me to see what we now both know: the labyrinth is unfinished. There is still something outside and something more beyond.

Gor must hear this, too.

But I do not say it. Because now the Caretakers have come.

"Take this for me," I say and press my purple marble into Gor's sweaty fist. "Put in my bunk. To the side. I have a spot . . . a hidden spot. Where I stash away such things. You'll see."

Gor looks at me with sudden sorrow. I wish we'd had more time to talk.

This thought remains: *We need more time.*

The Caretakers care nothing for our conversation. I'm not even sure they hear. I mean, they have no need for sound. They drag me hesitant and contrary far away from Gor. They bear me down the hall. We pass the room I almost always go, and I quake with sure and rising dread.

Once, I would demand an answer: "Where am I going? Where are you taking me? What happens now?" But I know better. There is no point in questioning those who can't or will not speak. So I quaver and tremble, and in cold sweats, I sadly guess: this must be the end.

They convey me to some distant chair and bind me down.

There will be no more threads to follow and no more hidden halls to find. This now is all and almost gone.

I come to, still in the chair. Have I been here long? I cannot say.

The rumbling in my stomach says it must be supper.

My feet ache. My head feels clear. My thoughts are still as crystal lakes.

When the bindings slip away, I flex my fingers, shake my wrists. I notice that my knuckles are bloody, bruised, and sore. I lick the scabs. I taste the blood. Who hurt me? Did I hurt them, too?

I hope I hurt them, too.

Am I safe? I cannot say.

The Voice recites my code. It tingles through my spine. It calls me, suppertime. Gladness, I feel, to get my belly full. To see my Gor, who never misses meals.

The Caretakers wave me on. My feet carry me quick and sure to the nearest dining hall.

002
(1o1o)

I RELAX IN THE WARM DIN OF SUPPER AS RAPT CHILDREN DINE ON MEATY sludge. The Voice calls, and I obey. I take my tray. I sit with Gor as always. Or so I think. At any rate, this seat feels right. Gor looks unsurprised to see me, so I judge this right.

I tuck into my stew. I lick and swallow with hunger fierce. Then look up from my spoon-scraped bowl to see him watching me, wary like the forest deer, his meal almost untouched.

"What's bad?" I ask and, with my index finger, tap his forearm. "You not hungry?" But Gor is always hungry, yes? This boy loves supper. This child loves breakfast. As all rapt children do. I think.

"What happened?" he demands to know, unpleased. Brows furrow, knit. "The Caretakers took you away. Some long time. Like morning until now. What did they do?"

Morning is a word for time. I know this true. So is night. But I don't remember this story he tells. I call back toward morning, some other time, and it's blurred in swirls. Some times. Some days. Some thoughts. Some feels. I reach back for memory and find nothing, like stepping off a stair into the void.

That cliff-edge panic wells up sudden and throbbing and choking in my chest. I push it down. Not now. Not now.

"What happened?" I ask Gor, instead. Repeat it back. Hope he tells me. So I don't have to say the truth: I can't remember, I don't know. "What *did* they do?"

"They made you forget," Gor says. He knows.

I know. So no use pretending. But still, I have my dignity. I have my pride. And I think—or feel—this day is deeply off, this world is wrong, some poison in the real. By instinct, I play strong. Lest it all fall apart. "But I'm hungry still. Give me your stew?"

He pushes it toward me without a thought, but before I can taste, he takes my closest hand. He pries open my curled fingers. This opening is what I dread; I keep safe by staying closed. But into my open palm he drops something. It's polished round, lunar smooth, amethyst as elf's eyes. Damp from Gor's warm stubborn grasp.

"Marble," I say. This word I know.

"You gave it to me. You remember that?"

I wait, distressed, silent. I do not like this game.

"Do you remember who gave it to you?"

"You said I gave to you," I protest in injured tones, this game growing yet still worse.

"You said your sister gave it to you first," he continues on, persistent. This boy could roll a boulder up an endless hill. This stoic child could move the sky, I think, if given slow and single-minded time.

"Sister," I say. No other words. But gaze with desperate longing at this marble in my palm. Aware it holds all truth I don't. The way it pricks. The way it trembles. Teeny as a pebble, massive as the world. It tugs at my wounded, jumbled brain-space. It stabs my heart. My chest is full and filled with raging sorrow for things I cannot know.

"You keep it," Gor says.

"I gave to you."

"I give it back."

I would argue more, but this feels right. I can tell this marble's mine. It rests against my hand and in my heart just so. So I hold it firm.

Gor asks too many questions. Do I remember this? Do I remember that? He follows me from spot to spot, picking and fretting. The cul-de-sac? The rubber boots? The monarch butterfly?

Do I remember summer thunderstorms, pizza with pineapple and ham?

Climbing an oak tree? Tossing a Frisbee? Running through the sprinkler beneath the blue and cloudless sky?

Do I remember harvesters, ripping children limb from limb and spewing all that blood?

He says I said I traveled far across this structure. He says I said I have a sister and I found her. She did not know me, but I knew her.

He says I came to the end of a tunnel and I saw a hole and outside that hole was the world we knew. He says if there was one hole there must be two. He talks and talks. He will not let me rest.

All these words and things tug painful at my thoughts. There's all these feels I cannot countenance. I don't know all that came before. It comes in waves, these feels of love and pain and want and loss. Tied to nothing. Meaning nothing. Giving nothing.

Who is he, anyway? To say these things? To know it all?

"Stop talking," I tell him, almost striking out at his sturdy self, though he's bigger than me by some good inch or two. "Stop. Stop."

"But I have to know," he says, tenacious still. "We have to figure it out. You made me promise. Before all this. I promised you."

"Promised me what?"

"I know I promised."

"Sounds stupid though, for real."

"You might remember. Like memory duty. If we say these things enough."

"Because why? Who cares?"

"Because no other children know the way."

Come about, he has this plan. His plan is that we fly away. I lead him and some others, and out we go. To make our way in whatever world lies outside still. This place called home. He and me and my sister. He says her name is Tess. So we escape.

These thoughts make me shake with terror-pain. Just imagining, it gives me sour churning in my stomach, burbles in my throat, sweat-slick palms, and pain in all my limbs. So terribly afraid.

"Don't," I beg. "Don't say such things. It's dark out there. Forever. I don't want to talk." I can't explain to him this panic, but I guess he knows because he gets quiet, sulks and broods.

Who is he, anyway? To make these claims? To say such things?

I begin to think, *Is this my Gor?*

Perhaps, some other Gor. They took my own away as they did with all the rest. They took him somewhere else and placed instead this other, who looks and talks and smells the same. Who's almost Gor but not quite mine.

I watch suspicious, listen doubtful. His hair the same. His eyes the same. His freckles all. But still I question.

I wait for evidence, either way. If he is himself or some imposter, a hoax to make this manufactured world more skewed.

"What?" he says. "Lolo? What's this mean?"

I don't know what it means. Again, my thoughts and words have fled.

Then, there is this.

One summer night, like lilac wine. The velvet sky alight with stars. And Tess and I, arranged in the hammock, a balance just so. Toes in the grass. The singing crickets and creaking toads.

This night is something else. All dark. And then behind the willow tree, a rising, piercing light. A glow begins to fill the sky.

We crane our necks and look in wonder: the moon? But so much bigger than before.

This full moon, like whole milk, its size and brightness from some prehistoric age.

"It's the supermoon," my sister says and proceeds to talk of science things: ellipses, orbits, apogees. From 'neath the hammock, our Bentley emits a snore. This numbing story bores him, too.

In the hammock, like a cradle beneath the spreading, beaming light, just cool enough the breeze, we sway and sway. I rub my bare feet in our puppy's fur, massage his flank with pink-painted toes. He likes this and leans in with contented pant.

It comes to me: how many dogs, how many girls, how many moons? So many nights beneath the stars. Since millennia and more before. This unbroken chain of love. All we need is fire's light.

In this life, I care for him, my Bentley. In other lives, he cares for me. We're born. We die. We're born again. All of this has happened. And all of this will happen still. Eternal recurrence. And together, us. We hold each other up. In this life and the next. In the future and the past. Still this.

I reach to hold my sister's hand.

She's gone.

The willow tree blots out the moon. I realize now it's dark and far more dark than night. The street lamps doused. The house lights out. The light from cities near and far all dimmed. The flickering world blown out like a girl blows out a candle.

It's not the willow tree; it's the lunar eclipse. The moon is blotted out with blood.

The back screen door is banging in the wind.

And Bentley stands in the corner of the yard, his rump to me, his head tossed back, barking loud and *fierceful* as he can to chase away this wretched moon.

I go toward the banging door. The black house. The home where monsters live.

The dog still barks.

Someone is calling me from inside the house. A voice I know but fear. With words I understand but hate.

Some languages are best forgotten.

So I'm stuck—afraid of stepping forward. Afraid of moving back.

There is someone behind me. Someone breathing very quiet, like they don't want to be heard.

I breathe more quiet still.

Someone rests their hand upon my shoulder.

I do not make a peep.

No one protects me. This idea was just a ruse. I'm all alone through all the worlds with no one to watch, no guardian to keep me safe.

I never learned to scream.

In my bunk, I try to sleep. For some few nights, no nightmares threatened. Those nights are past. The dark dreams are back, full force.

I am above. Gor below. Between my shallow breaths, I listen for his own. He's still awake, I think. I still don't know who is he, really. I don't know how long we've been doing this, how long we've been in this cycle, remembering, forgetting, remembering again.

How many lives have we lived inside this structure? This world could be brand-new or ancient-old. I've come to see I have no way to know.

"Lolo?" says Gor.

"Gor?" says I.

"You awake?"

"Yes."

"Can I come up?"

"Okay."

A moment later, his shaggy head poking up the ladder, his gangly body swinging onto my slim bunk. He crouches at the end, his nubby knees crushed against my cold bare feet.

He gazes at the sketches. I tell from his expression, he knows already of these rust-red etchings. He's seen these diagrams before.

My walls are covered with these desperate scrawlings. Images I recognize. Others I don't. Since I came back to myself, I've seen them every night. I'd rather not. Like all, they whisper nightmares I'd soon not know. I sleep in the shadow of these cryptic emblems and try not to toss and turn.

But Gor, with his forever pestering—of course, this child insists. "Do you remember these?"

"I suppose," I say, doubtful. But in a way, I do. I know I knew them once. They exude this feral stink that lingers in my heart, these primal fumes of loss and love. I can't deny. I've traced them with my fingertips a time or two, searching echoes of past movements.

"You remember writing these?" he says. "You know how you made them?"

"I wrote these?" I say. "I made these." This I think feels right. Agree with what he says.

"You made these. You told me. You wrote these all. You did it to remember."

"I did it to remember."

"You know how you made them?" he asks again.

"I wrote them."

"You wrote with blood. You told me all of this. Before. You told it all. I knew. I know. You told me how you stole a syringe, carved yourself, wrote with blood, left this message. To find your sister. To find your Tess."

I watch him more suspicious than ever. These lies. They feel like lies. I would never do such things.

Or would I? Yes, perhaps, I would.

So this new thought comes to me, *I am Lolo. I have a sister. I am a child who discovered writing, and I gave up my own blood.*

"Give me your arm," Gor says, and grudging, ready to whip and strike like a snake, I let him at my limb. Afraid he might prick me with a needle. Perhaps, this boy's insane.

Instead, he pushes up my sleeve. In the nighttime dim of night, he looks hard at my skin. Searching for scars he won't find. I've looked there myself. For reasons, I guess, I can't quite say. My flesh is all unbroken.

"You had those scars before," he says to me. "You did. I know. I'm almost sure."

Yes, we all are almost sure.

I look at these crude etchings. Something like a swing set. Something like a dog. Something like an explosion in the sky. Some scribbled number-codes and emblems, symbols, too, I know are signs across the structure. This all meant something, I suppose, but now, the meaning's gone.

Perhaps, if I'm slow and careful, cunning still, I will remember all. Decipher what it means.

"Can I lie here?" Gor says and gestures to my pillow and the space beside me.

I nod, wordless, and he stretches out side-to-side with me beneath the scratchy coverlet. I curl on my side, this movement feeling right. His front to me. My back to him. I see we fit just right. I feel, whatever else may be forgotten, my self knows his self.

My panicked breathing slows. My heartbeat finds its rhythms. My every cell is settling down. And this feels safe. This feels like home.

So I trust the things I do not know and follow my snoring Gor into our sleep.

I wake in the room to the sound of swings. This remains, whatever else—the creaking, shrieking sigh and groan. It presses in and presses in. So many unhinged chains, flapping and soaring in harsh gales. It makes me crazy. It makes me fear for things unknown, which makes it all the worse. I don't know why this sound gives me such terrors.

I thrash and squirm against the binds. I scream for help. Until my throat is sore. While the worthless Caretakers stand in corners, all remote, like they can't be bothered much to hear. Or perhaps, they simply can't. They see, though, my distress and make no move toward my aid. Just let me throw myself against the chains until I'm bruised and sore while the loathsome sound grows louder, coming closer in.

"Make it stop!" I shout, but they care nothing for my fury.

Stop, it does. I pant in sudden silence. Limp with all the feels.

Next thing, they're wheeling out the science cart. They fill a syringe with some liquid. Inject it in my self. I yelp at the prick, but it hardly hurts a bit. If Gor can be believed, I'm much tougher than that. The fluid pumps in. My veins expand. My mind tilts outward. Some minutes pass—or longer perhaps—I can't exactly say for sure. Whatever it is, this fluid brings the bliss. They give me this forgetting drug, and in this moment, it's sweet.

When the swings slash at my head again—not just the sound but sight too, like I'm flat on my chest against the ground, collapsed against some nubby grass while chains shriek in the wind—when all this noise and fury descend on me, I'm not afraid.

I'm safe inside this bubble of my brain. It's not so bad. This memory returns, declawed, defanged. They rewrite it all.

Nothing's real, and nothing's true. And on and on it goes.

We remake the world, Gor and I. At night, in darkness when it finally seems we're free, when the Voice is stilled, when the Caretakers' webbed lids drift shut upon their black-orb eyes—then, all rapt children sleep, and the darkness lets us dream.

We remake the world in a frenzy of telling, rebuild all history from scraps of stories, snatches of memories, half-remembered dreams. We choose our own memory duty and this is it. For us and us alone.

We whisper, whisper, and he tells me, and I tell him. It's not like breakfast where children speak their dreams. There's room to bend, there's room to build, we know now we can create all truth if we just work hard enough. All it takes is symmetry. So we reach on deep.

But Gor's dreams of late are fears. He knows about the black house. He's been there, too.

"What's inside?" I say, though I'm not quite sure I want to know.

"What's *not* inside?" he asks.

I'm still afraid to touch the door.

But what if, he says, *what if it's not the way we thought?* Those idyllic glimpses of a life unmarred by fear. Those simple visions of the departed world: a filter tinted emerald and turquoise, picket fences where the sun always shines and the stars are bright and the song of an ice cream truck is the song of crickets is the song of dawn-herald birds is the song of gentle rain against the roof. *This perfect lie,* he says, *and now, I see it too.* This lie that held the sinkholes. This lie that held black houses. This lie that held the blood.

Too bright. Too innocent. This world could not be real. It's dangerous fiction, and it's hiding something; it always has. So what's it hiding now?

Something in the closet, he says. He says it goes on far deeper and far longer than it should. So dark you cannot see your hand. Your trembling candles fail. This now, the void. This infinite, it clambers out. Sometimes the brass knob rattles—the howl wants inside. *Let me in,* it says. This flimsy door can hardly hold the darkness back.

But I'm hidden, too, I say. And this I know. I sometimes huddled. In that dark space beneath the coats, the only place that's safe. No room for dogs. No room for sisters. No room for monsters. *Why do I hide? Because I'm not safe. Because they've always tried to hurt me. Because this dumb child I've always been and always will be.*

Who hurts? The Caretakers? But this was before.

"Who took care of us before the Caretakers?" I ask.

This, Gor doesn't want to say.

"Tell me," I say. "Tell me. Why can't I know?"

"This just my rememberings," he says. "Could be as lies as all the rest."

"Tell me, now," I say.

"There have always been taller ones, stronger ones, ones who knew what we didn't know," Gor says, hesitant. "Before the structure. Before the labyrinth. Before the Caretakers. They've always been there. They've always hurt us."

"Before the Caretakers?"

"We called them parents."

A pain stabs deep within my flank. The pain of being cut, again, again, so the Caretakers can carelessly extract the elixirs they cultivate inside. These nectars for a ravaged world. I give, again, again, but not like—Tess?

"We have to get away," Gor says. He says it every night now. "You said yourself.

You told me. There's this outer edge. This hole ripped in the skin. And outside, something else. Our only hope. That space is free."

"I can't. I can't."

"You went there once. You said. You promised me," he says.

"I don't remember."

"You walked and walked."

These thoughts are rough. I can't think—I won't think—I won't go. I grit my teeth against this maze. I hate this nausea. I refuse to navigate. I detest this panic in my gut. I abhor the labyrinth. I won't go. He can't make me. I'd rather suffer. I'd rather stay.

"This map," he says and points again at the etchings on my wall. "I'll figure it out if you won't. I'll crack the code."

"Get out," I urge. "Get out."

He insists he'll translate this, my private language that not even I still know.

"Worst child," I hiss with graveled whispers. "Get down."

He gets down. By next breakfast, again we're friends. Still, his persistence doesn't end.

The swings are shrieking in the hyperactive wind. The chains are grinding. The metal's creaking.

But this now, I feel nothing.

I inventory the contents of my feels, I comb through pulses of my heart, like an age-stooped crone picking over her ocean-polished shells. There is no fear. It's been erased.

A silver cord is severed. Now, I'm free but also bereft, devoid of whatever it was I sometimes felt, that heartbroken story that it held.

The Voice speaks as always: *What do you feel? What do you think? How did it make you—*

And grilling on and on.

Are you afraid? Do you remember? Did you forget?

How does it make you—

But nothing. It's empty. No longer charged.

And thus contented, the Caretakers set me free.

In this bubble, our dreams bleed together, intertwined.

Gor remembers a place called Kaspar's Play Place, where all good children begged to venture. The tables low to the ground, the chairs all sculpted from some rainbow glass. And inside this cage, a maze where we could play. He tells of trays, not like our own. The food all slick-grease and salty-sweet. The milkshakes from a straw. The fries burning all our fingertips. The neon-orange nectar staining all our lips. A child's hot and sticky feast. And sweet and spicy sauces in so many plastic tubs.

I remember different. I remember Kaspar's by the beach. This rickety stand buffeted by salty breeze. This whole strip whipped by wind that tangles in my hair. Tess and I, we stand on tiptoes at the window. This hut looks like it's not been cleaned in decades, maybe more. Thick with salt and dust and rust. But ice cream—oh, so many flavors. Peppermint is pink and so is bubblegum. Pistachio is green and so is daiquiri ice. Tess likes peanut-butter fudge. Double-scoops, each.

I scarf it down, Gor says. *I scarf it all. Onions, pickles, ketchup, too.* Fast as he can. So he can play. He scrunches up the crinkled papers, smeared and stained with grease, slurps all orange pop for extra juice, dumps all trash, rockets up. "Take off your shoes!" Of course. He climbs into this maze, this cage . . .

It's hard to choose, I say. But choose we do. Then sit on bench all sprawled in baking sun, licking cones fast as we can before sweet drippings drench our teeny hands. Eager Bentley lying, always, at our feet, intent to catch what drips our tongues may miss. With his blackberry jowls against his golden fur, he does seem to be grinning. His leash looped loose around my wrist; he has no need to stray, just lies and pants and grins in hopes of sweet vanilla ice cream and crunchy waffle cone. His paws all scuffed with salt. This beast must have a bath. Pop music blares from stereos while stupid hot rods drag race *vrooming* down the street.

Then Gor beside, too. Somehow on this bench. Noshing his strawberry scoops. Happy as can be. As he belongs and always has.

Then meeting in this tunnel, Gor says. *I climbing up. You climbing down. Tight. Too tight for both to pass. So which way should we go?*

Which way is best? I say.

Whichever way leads out.

We crawl together.

This tunnel's longer than we thought. And getting longer. Growing faster as we crawl. And getting tighter. Darker too. The darkness always knows.

My sky is darker, too. That flawless blue now dank with clouds. And Bentley growls. He knows always, too. The clouds roll in. The coldness shivers in our skin. The banks of clouds bear closer and closer. Like the chaos behind Gor's bedroom closet door. Like the black house, the back door always banging in the wind. The wind is always shrieking, too.

This tunnel is suffocating us.

This tidal wave is drowning us.

Forget. Forget. Forget.

If only we could.

In my bunk at the top of our bubble, Gor questions. He points at this. He points at that. Saying, what was this? Do you remember? What's the feel when you see those words? When you see those numbers, too?

I tell him, "I had a sister. I had a dog."

He tells me, "I lived in a falling-down house on a gutted street where the weeds grew high in neglected patches of dead grass and Styrofoam trash drowned in the clogged drains."

I tell him, "Sometimes, my house turns black. When out, I can't see in. When in, I can't see out. There are hidden secrets there. And gravity's agonizing pull . . ."

He tells me, "The shades are drawn on fetid afternoons, my mother stretched pale across the couch, her dead face flickering in the TV's lurid glow. With my heel, I grind the crumbs into the carpet; with my heel, I grind the crumbs . . ."

But still, joy in survival. We could escape. Maybe even live.

And then? What happened then?

A day when it all changed.

The day the Caretakers came down.

This day differs from now to now. Sometimes morning, sometimes night; sometimes sudden, sometimes slow.

He analyzes my fingertips. He points them to his own. This much we decipher, easy as pie: those symbols, numbers, emblems, they hold some meaning. They are some map. They could point the way.

We could still escape. Maybe even live.

And then? What happens next?

One morning soon at breakfast. It seems real quiet now, like not so many children. The ones still there don't talk as much, keeping to themselves, silent and suspicious, as I was once, too. No wills to break the silence. The talk is furtive, sidelined by the chewing and the clink of forks.

The Caretakers sit at the four corners, as always. They look alike. They are identical, mostly, four pillars. We've come to ignore them, though always uneasily.

Most days they pick a few of us for memory duty. But not today.

Today is something new.

More Caretakers than we've ever seen before pour into this room like ants. They come and come, a horde of them. Until there are nearly more of them than us. Where did they find them all? Where were they hiding? Do they hatch like eggs? For that matter—do us children, too?

The Caretakers herd all kids together. Without speaking. With gestures only. We don't know what they want. We don't know how to move. We almost stampede. But they push and pull us forward with their cold, hard fingers. They force us into this stiff formation. One long line, they force us into two-by-two. This line snakes around the dining hall, through scattered chairs.

"What's happening? What happens next? Why now? Why us? You take us where?" We query all these things. And shake and tremble with fear because we know by now that, when such things happen, the outcome is never joy. This echoes days that we've forgotten, but their shadows haunt us still.

Of course, the pale creatures don't answer. Their eyes elude our gaze. It's almost like they're dead.

In this now, the Voice could speak, explain it all. The Voice could give us comfort, at least try to reassure.

All we want is just to know and try to understand. How did we get here? Why did we come? What do they want? Why won't they stop?

But knowing is what they rob us of the most.

They usher us forward. Out of this dining room where breakfast is. We falter and hesitate and stumble, but they push us forward. Through dark halls, like the one Gor says I once traversed when I fled to search for my lost sister. The halls are crude and somehow incomplete. The ground rough to our bare feet. The green lights glowing from the walls.

In my head, I try to force a map, but this maze is senseless. Like its elements are transient. Like its building blocks are restive and always in flux.

Come about after this forced marching, we find ourselves in a strange and unfamiliar hall. All rows and rows of seats, again makeshift and new. An odor of fresh-built material I almost recognize but can't quite place. All seats face toward a massive wall, all blank. We file in without a sound, mute and afraid.

Gor is beside me and has been all along since we first sat in our usual spots at breakfast. Again, we sit where we're told. He grabs my hand. I squeeze hard, squeeze back. We can hear the muffled sound of crying, rising all around. There is no cause to cry. Not yet, at least. But any change from our routines is enough to put some into a tizzy. We have no past with which to grasp the new. It's all alarming, overwhelming, vast. So some rapt children cry.

A sound rings like a trumpet blast. The wall ahead becomes a screen. The screen begins to play.

It feels like faded, ancient footage, the colors all washed out as a static crackle pervades beneath it all. Not black-and-white but close and, like the Caretakers, all silent.

A view from the sky. The sprawling cities. The networks of roads. The green-and-brown patchwork of endless fields. Zooming in, closer and closer still.

Flanked by phalanxes of spaceships, everywhere and all. More than I could count. In slow motion, they seem to overcome the world.

Then still photos. Flashing on and on.

The labyrinth rises. The structure accretes and coheres, built by teeming nanite swarms. A ramp is built from ground to sky.

The children marching, two by two.

Is this real? Is this what happened?

It feels so false. It feels so fake.

Nothing like those memory duties we've done since always in rooms alone, swamped in the feels. This is flat and silent. No touch. No sound. No smell. It does not persuade as real at all. So why is it here? What does it mean?

Perhaps, this is what happened.

It doesn't feel right.

But what else could?

Gor leans close to me and whispers in my ear as the final frames stutter to black. "You see that world? You see that ramp? It goes both ways. It goes to ground. We find it. Take it out. Escape. For real. We do."

"You're crazy, Gor," I whisper back. My heart-chest fights my mind-head fights my leaping-dancing gut. I want to go. I'm terrified. I'm desperate longing. I'm . . . I feel I used to know much more, who and what this Lolo is. It may take some time to find. I discovered writing, this I know. I have a purple marble. I'm with Gor, and he with me . . . "I'm afraid," I tell him as simple and straightforward as I know.

"But you were bravest first," he says, and though I can't know in this now why he insists such things, I hold it true.

Lolo, bravest first.

We notice next at breakfast: not so many children as before, and those who remain are extra-fearful. Stained wells beneath their eyes point to nightmares and sleepless nights. The emptying rooms of our laboratory home, the distant hallways—these abandoned spaces echo with hoarse whispers. A shadow has fallen. We don't know why. I don't know why. If Gor knows, he cannot say. Something's happened. Or something's coming.

As this darkness gathers, we all retreat into our bruised and broken selves. We want to ask, "What's bad? What nightmare comes?" But fears breed silence. So we wait. We wait.

The Voice summons one away and then another. They don't come back. These once-rapt children won't return.

Sometimes, they send us to the room with unmoving bikes. In this room, we perch on hard and narrow seats, grasp our sticky handle bars, pedal fast and furious upon these wheels affixed. It makes us glow and sweat.

It feels awfully good to move, to lose myself and all my terrors inside my swelling breath. These machines remind some of darling memories, riding bikes in summer twilight as cicadas hummed with all their might and bats wheeled overhead.

This pedal room is filled with vibrations, building hums of children all intent upon their pumping knees.

So yes, pedaling makes me glad. I like it here. But last few times (or last few days), some sessions I have noticed, this room is not exactly like it was. I remember it bigger. I thought more children, more pedal machines, more rows of wheels.

"Do you think?" I ask Gor through puffing breath. "It used to be bigger? More? I thought?"

Gor nods. Gor shrugs. He doesn't say "No."

I see he sees it, too.

Somehow, the walls are closing in, now tighter than before.

One day, it's undeniable. One wall is getting closer.

I climb from my machine, and all rapt children watch—for most, I think it never occurs that they could choose to disobey. There are times the Voice commands, and those commands we are compelled to follow or pain and sickness rise all over.

But other times . . . the Caretakers don't necessarily hold these magics on us. We can disrespect. We can rebel.

I climb from my machine, aware of all their eyes on me, and I slow approach this slippery wall that refuses to stay put.

I rest my fingertips against it, slow and hesitant. It feels like other walls.

Which learns me something—this wall can move, and all walls seem the same, so I think all walls can move. This structure is in ever-flux, flowing halls and floors and rooms. The maze is maze because it's constant change.

Gor dismounts his pedals, too. The rest of the rapt children pedal and watch close. I feel my hands across the wall, searching for something I cannot know—a gap, a crack, a place of weakness. Some hint of why this wall is restless.

Some facts I know: not all doors are easy seen. Some are hidden, wearing odd camouflage for reasons of their own. Some doors—

I think these thoughts with ease as if I've thought them all before. They flow along some once-carved path. And startle me. Pull at my heart. I think, *There's something there.*

I start from where I am. Pacing slow along the wall, gentle fingers searching.

Reaching high, reaching low. Looking with my hands.

I *have* done this before. I know more memories than I could ever find.

Too many lost lives.

Gor is helping too, searching with his fingers.

Is it me? Is it him? Is it the labyrinth itself, speaking to us best it can? I don't know. Not now. Not yet. But the wall turns clear. We fall back, startled. Our fingertips leave smudges on this wall that's now a window. We peer through the glass. It's clear as day.

On the other side, all children, just like us, perched on their machines, their backs to us, pedaling. We stare at their hunched shoulders, their pumping legs. Just like us. Perhaps, the ones we lost.

On our side of the glass, more children climb from their machines. More rapt ones approach the glass.

On their side, the first child takes notice. He glances over shoulder—stops pedaling—and looks around again.

I gasp. I cannot help myself.

This child has no mouth.

I gasp, and this gasp draws all the more to us.

This child climbs down from his machine and walks to us. He peers at us from through this glass. Just like us, almost. But where his mouth should be, all sealed. The flesh clean as my once-scarred forearm, now like a baby's bottom. Smooth and pale expanse of lower face.

Somehow, he calls them on his side. Since he has no mouth, he cannot speak. But more of his fellows, some girls, some boys, clad in pajamas like our own, with heads not shorn but shaved, all dismounting their machines, moving as one, this single-minded horde. Moving in unison and drawn as if by some force outside themselves.

They swarm the glass. They're pressing close.

I see one, at least, she puts her fingers on the glass. This sight familiar. I see her fingertips. I see the code. The first emblem is my own. I file this away.

On our side of the glass all children are stampeding too. Banging. Shouting. Screaming. Pandemonium broken loose.

I must admit. I am Lolo, bravest first, but I do some screaming too.

In this loud screaming, scampering rush, Gor grabs my hand, or I grab his. We're holding tight.

Children are running every which way.

The Caretakers are here now, wielding their zappers. But they can't zap each one fast enough. Too many running. Too many bolting. The children are like panicked animals on the plains. The zapping makes them shout and scream, and it all grows all the worse.

I am Lolo, the child who discovered writing, the girl who launched a riot.

Gor and I run. Not caring which direction. Just panting desperate to leave that horror behind, those children without mouths. Just trying to escape. We flee the pedal room, pound down some long and twisty halls, and sprint on. We go beyond the edge of this laboratory home.

I find I'm running first, running ahead, as if I know the way. Maybe I do.

We run until we reach the quiet and the dark. We find some hidden cubby, like a tunnel inside another tunnel's hold. We duck inside. We crawl deep as we can, hidden from any peering eyes.

In that darkness, we pant and choke and wheeze. Try to catch our breaths. This horror is the worst yet. It can't be real. But is it? It might be.

We're holding tight. Arms wrapped around. Fingers pressed so hard they leave red marks, and our fingertips go bloodless white.

Some time goes by. We try to breathe.

Dark and closeness, hot breath, clenched hands. They're all that keeps us safe. Perhaps, they're all that is.

Some times goes by. We stay in this cubby. Afraid to move. Afraid to leave.

Why do I hide? Because I'm not safe.

"Do you remember blanket forts?" Gor says. "I wish I had one now."

And I do, I remember. I think about how Tess and I used to build. Dogged, dragging each dining room chair into place. Then the couch cushions, the walls. Draping faded, tattered quilts, pieced with humility and stitched with longing by great-aunts we never knew; positioning scruffy, fuzzy afghans knitted by grandmothers with stiff fingers. The dining room table, another room. So warm and dim inside those folds.

We crawled on bare knees. We positioned ourselves just so. We packed snacks for our hideaway, and Bentley begged to join in too, and though his eager wagging tail and careless snout kept dismantling our house, we could not say no. His gentle snuffle nose. Trolling 'neath the dining table for crumbs.

We sucked from plastic straws poked into juice boxes and crunched on salty crackers 'til they turned to paste. We stayed together, safe in the warm air of each other and the stink of dog. The sun glowed through the holes in the knitted blanket's weave.

"The sun?" Gor says. "But it's night. It's dark . . ."

"You were there?"

"Yes," he says. "I was there. Of course. I'm always there."

Another word for time is *always*.

And the blanket fort inside the dining room of our childhood home becomes a tent on a hilltop where we camped far away from here. The three of us: me, Tess, Gor. We build our blanket nests inside the tent. We build a fire outside and gather 'round as the glowing flames make our cheeks flush pink.

The crickets sing, and the bullfrog chants, and the owl hoots from somewhere far. We watch the drifting clouds.

Contentedly, we tell our stories, we share our memories, we count the cold, bright stars. Here, far away from everything, the sky is darker than you dream, and the stars shine with the purest, fiercest light. Every constellation glows in all its points and holds the symmetries of every ancient myth.

Then the stars begin to disappear.

One by one, the stars black out. Less stars. More dark. All blotting out. Some force extinguishes them all.

We watch, we wait, sad but not surprised because we knew it couldn't last.

The alien spaceships are filling every last square inch of sky. The fleet is cutting us three children off from the light of every star.

It always ends this way.

"Okay, okay," I say, hoarse and sorrowful into the darkness. "This time. Before it's too late. Before we both forget. Before they take our mouths and we forget how to speak."

"Before it's too late," Gor echoes.

"Let's go. We'll go."

"We'll bring our sister."

"Of course. We'd never leave without our sister."

So we go. With stiff and sore and aching limbs, we pry ourselves from out this hidey-hole we found. We set off into the labyrinth.

We go to rescue Tess.

003
(1o1o)

FIRST ALONG THE PATH, I FIND THE FORK JUST DROPPED THERE, A prickly silhouette against the dimly glowing wall. I squat down low. Look where it's dropped. As if on purpose. But also with some nonchalance.

I lift this fork, turn it over, analyze it careful. These almost-familiar tines, snagging something in my brain.

Along the handle—a narrow streak of dark-dried blood.

I show to Gor.

"You left this here?" he asks, uncertain.

I might have done. Might be a message sent from me to me. Or perhaps, just is. But who strolls a long-dead passage, dropping bloody forks?

"We'll see," I say. "We'll see."

On we go, treading soft in nondescript tunnels. All look the same. Aggressively the same, in fact, so much you could begin to doubt. You might fear you've walked the same stretch twice or far more times than that.

But we do not see the fork.

Instead, we come upon a scrap of cloth. This tattered strip is soft and white, like undershirts. It's also marked with the faint smear of blood.

So perhaps, I did. This trail. Left by me. For me. Or left by me for someone else. Or left by someone else for me.

Or left by someone else for someone else, nothing to do with me, Gor, our sister Tess . . . but this flawed scrap of map is what we have, so we follow it with care.

Faster now. Spurred, excited by the bits and bobs.

A couple blocks, like the ones we use to build in the room where rapt children play. A couple still-wrapped sweets. (No worries; no ants inside this structure, nor any other living things.) Some further spoons and forks. Some puzzle pieces, forever incomplete.

These hopeful objects point us to where the paths turn and help us choose our way.

This path of crumbs.

We follow their trail, hoping they'll lead, not knowing how or why or where.

And this is all.

'Til we come to the new emblem, the foreign symbol, which I remember still.

These rapt children sit all arrayed before a screen, like us on the day they led us to the film. These children have no chairs: they sit and lay and sprawl on kid-sized cushions, relaxed and half-reclined. All wear pajamas, blue. Their faces remain all blank and endless, raptured gaze. They watch the screen. It plays.

Gor and I creep in, all silent and unnoticed. These children, we think, are none too smart. Perhaps, always and ever drugged, remain in blissed-out, gorgeous state, like me sometimes in memory room.

The screen plays not a story but only visions of a place. The place is an ancient forest, all canopies of verdant green. Among the tops of tallest trees are kaleidoscopic tents, gracious slung between the branches. The brightest birds flit back and forth, calling out with joyous songs. Monkeys swing from branch to branch with their clever little hands. Children scamper with them along the woven ropes that bind their homes.

These rapt children love this scene. They watch entranced and never glance away. Though some do nibble nervous at their fingertips or chew the frayed ends of their hairs or suck their thumbs, the ancient forest demands their gaze.

I fall into it, too—the screen's hypnotic, all that quiet noise of birds and kids, of rustling leaves, of crawling insects, of gentle tropic rain. All those vibrant colors. All this life. I want to live inside it. I want to be there, always.

I see Gor falling too. That raptured stillness.

But determined, we pull our gaze away. We must find Tess.

We crawl and creep among the beanbag thrones and don't disturb the children whose eyes stay on the screen.

And there she is—legs crossed, arms, too—sat against the wall, off on the very right. Head tilted slightly back, lips parted, face blank as she watches the forest.

We sit on either side of her. We whisper quietly; no Caretakers must come. I take the right side. Gor the left. We take her hands.

"Listen. You're our sister. We're here to save you. Come with us."

She slowly turns her gaze to us, eyes blurry and unfocused, and gently shakes her head.

"Yes, you must," we say, but she shakes her head again. Not mad. Nor even scared. Just slowly, gently, *No*. Like not even sure we're real, we're there.

I press the violet marble in her hand.

She stares at it for quite some while then closes her fingers tight. This time she nods her head. "Okay," she says. "Okay."

I stroke her soft wrist. I touch her hair. There are so few words we share. It's the only way I know to say. But love. *But love.*

"It's safe," I whisper. "It's okay. We're friends. We're sisters. I'll keep you safe."

"It's okay," Gor says. "We'll keep you safe."

Slowly, Tess turns pliable, this sweet and trusting soul. She starts to smile. She lets us pull her up and pull her forward. We trip on feet and legs of children who barely notice as we creep away. Tess follows like the smallest child. She keeps hold of the marble. We walk along.

We call her Tess—again, again—as we pad along the corridor. "Tess?" she says at last. "It's me. I'm called *Tess*."

"Yes," Gor and I bubble with all this joy. Happier than you know. She's coming around to us, remembering it all.

"Where are we going?" she asks. Still gripping tight my hand.

"We're getting out. We'll leave this place."

"We go to the trees?" she says. "The place with trees? Tess loves the birds. I love the birds. I love the trees."

"Maybe," Gor says. "Maybe?"

"Maybe," she repeats and seems content. Maybe maybe is good enough.

But she stops dead. Stands in perfect corpselike stillness. She drops the marble. Drops my hand. Goes stiff all over.

A quick sharp cry, her face goes blank, her jaw goes slack. Her eyes roll backward in her head.

"What's going on?" Gor says. "What's happening to her? Sister? Are you okay?"

"I don't know," I say, terrified. "I don't know"—I'm shaking her, gripping her shoulders—"Tess? Tess? Are you alright? What's wrong?"

She's absent a moment and comes to. Stares at me with fearful eyes and, gasping, yanks away. She glances around, wild and frantic, at the empty hall, the dark blank walls, the dimly guiding glow. "Where is?" she yammers. "Who are? What now?"

"Shh, shh," I say. "It's okay. It's okay. Tess. You're our sister. Gor. Lolo. You're safe."

So we stop to stroke and comfort, to talk in soft and gentle tones, to explain it all again. To rescue the purple marble where it dropped and press it back into her palm. This seems to make her calm, this and this alone.

We walk and walk some more. She's following along. She's calm now. She's asked about the trees. "Maybe," Gor says, and good enough.

But then—

It happens, all again. This seizure breaks. It yanks her under. And when she comes to surface, she's panicked, flailing, lost. She's lost whatever came before. And we tell it all again . . .

"Why does it happen to her, not us?" Gor asks. "Why just Tess?"

"And perhaps, all children in her place," I muse, the way they all seemed half-asleep and half-awake, sitting tight in that twilight room, watching the same film as it endless looped, the same six, seven minutes that scrolled again, again.

"But how did we escape such fate?"

"Did we escape?" I question. Because who knows how long we remain like this, unscathed, or what happened before or happens next?

"For now," he says. "I guess for now," which I'll admit is good enough.

I say this vague conviction, "Something in their heads, I guess. They do something to their heads. So when it comes, they hear it inside. Like the Caretakers—no ears, they somehow hear the Voice."

I think on this and feel a sudden sympathetic pain. At the base of my skull, where my cranium meets my neck, I wince at some imaginary twinge. My fingers fly to there. I feel for scar. No scar, of course; just skin.

This goes on, and this goes on.

Then we reach a door.

Only one can open the door. It's Tess. Her fingers. Her gentle fingers know it. Or it knows her. The door fades away.

On the other side is a vast, unending darkness and, snaked across it, a narrow needle of an endless bridge.

Below us, the wall drops sheer, like a cliff.

We stand at the verge.

Ahead, the catwalk is a gossamer thread stretched beneath two worlds. Below, a yawning chasm, the black and everlasting hole. Behind, the maze.

There is no hurt to this step. Whatever training kept us close to home, it dissipated long ago. We are as rapt to this world as the day we were first new.

"Who goes first?" Gor asks.

"I go," I say. "I go." Lolo, bravest first. I'll lead the way.

I take the step. I venture first one footfall and again, two. The bridge is sound.

They follow behind.

My elbow bumps the unseen rail: there, but transparent, no thicker than a gleam in darkness. I do my best, I don't look down. There is no ground. It drops away longer and deeper and darker than my eyes can see.

As does the wall, as does the maze . . .

Try not to look. Walk forward. One step. Another. Tess behind me. Gor the last. Walking in one line, trying not to look.

I cannot see the end; this bridge just might go on forever. The pale glow fades to dim. Ahead, darkness . . . we walk and walk. One step. Another.

"You know," Gor says. "You notice?"

"Uh-huh?" I say.

"Yes, brother?" says Tess.

"It's Tess," Gor says. "No blanks. Since we stepped out on the bridge. She's all remembered."

"You're right," I say with an ocean's rush of joy. "She remembers. You remember, Tess?"

"I remember," she says. "We walk and walk . . . we're getting out. We're leaving. We're getting free."

"Yes," I say, and "Yes," says Gor.

"We're going home," I say again, trilling all over with the sheer and far-fetched joy.

"We're going to the trees," Tess says, blissful. No one contradicts. Because for all we know, we are. We know not what's outside, except our broken memories, our jumbled dreams.

"But look," she says, pausing. She stands and turns back toward the place we came. We also turn to look, reaching nervously for the see-through wall that stops our fall, hoping it remains.

We've walked far enough to get a wider glimpse, and the epic view astounds. The picture's almost too shocking to take in.

We walked out of a wall. That wall is just a tiny piece of cube in a vast and massive city suspended in vaster and more massive darkness still. We lived our whole lives in that cube, believing it the world.

The cube is checkered, patterned with stripes. Some bits transparent, some opaque. The see-through parts reveal so much: hundreds of floors, all filled with halls and labs and rooms, and Caretakers and children—too many and too much to count.

Too far, too small, to make out faces or recognize a thing or place. We only get the sense of it.

This place is so much bigger than we knew.

We keep on keeping on.

We walk. We pass more cubes. Far from us. Near to us. Some grinding ever closer.

We sit and rest. We walk, and the bridge ends.

Another wall, another tunnel, another maze—and some despair, for us, because who knows if it ends?

But having come this far, all we can do is continue on.

My sister's becoming someone else. Her thoughts are piling up on thoughts. She starts to talk and talk. She asks and asks: where did we come from, how did we end up here in this structure, and what came before? How did we find each other? And Gor besides? How long have we been here? Who are the Caretakers? Why them? Why us? Why now?

We tell her all we know. But what we know is just enough to rankle. What we know is mostly all we don't. It seems most all mysteries still elude our grasps.

"I'm hungry. Are you hungry?"

Of course, this query could only come from Gor.

I'm hungry. My belly's grumbled for some time. "But I see no long table set and ready for our lunch, so don't know what there is to do but starve."

"Suppertime by now, I'd think," Gor says.

These walls, like tired charcoal, give no hint as to what part of day it is or how much time has passed.

"No Kaspar's Play Place either," I add, more nasty than before.

"I have candy, though," says Gor. What do you know? This child stops, pulls up his pajama top. Underneath, he's turned his soft undershirt into a bandage as he claims I once did to my arm. Tucked inside this makeshift pouch, he's hidden some flat foods.

Tess and I laugh and laugh while Gor pulls out bacon strips, all cold and plastic, and candy bars, somewhat squashed, and paper-wrapped sweets, and single-sliced, single-wrapped triangles of cheese. All edibles that appear often on our mealtime trays and only slightly less edible after their unlikely journey inside our brother's shirt.

"You go around like this always?" I question, laughing still. "Just hauling lunch?"

Sheepish, he begins to portion out the snacks, careful we all get enough.

"Just some recent times," he says. "Since we started talking how we'd flee. I saw that ramp . . . I hoped that soon . . . I thought it would be good to plan."

I might be Lolo, bravest first, but my Gor has got his strong points, too.

"That's smart," Tess said. "You thought ahead."

And walking on, we munch upon these sweets.

We reach a place, like none we've seen before.

A cube without symbols or emblems. A mess of hallways where the light glows a soft pink. We don't know how to go.

I feel this crawling feeling on the back of my neck. A tickle lodged between my shoulder blades that has me anxious and squirming in my skin.

Thinking, maybe this spot is where it's all about to end. We'll be caught by the Caretakers, who will carry us away back to anywhere. It's all bad, all.

But maybe not.

"Don't be afraid, little one," a small voice speaks. A small Voice. I whip around, startled. But Gor doesn't hear. And Tess doesn't hear. They trip along, oblivious. They hear nothing. "You'll find the way. You always do."

First time I hear the Voice inside my skull, like the Caretakers. So perhaps, it's all too late.

I think, that feel like fingers down my spine? That's what it feels like to come into the Voice's notice. That feel's the gaze of it. Turning all its thoughts on us.

These crazy thoughts. This crazy talk. I keep all to myself. We wander in the rose glow, like the womb of this world.

Then pass through a door—

This hall is vaster than a cathedral, and it's filled with rows and rows and rows of walls that almost reach the sky, and each one is built of tanks on tanks, and in these tanks bubbles pleasant fluid. In each tank, there floats a child.

Some girls, some boys, all naked, all alike, same face, same hair, same size, like all three of us. They float. They breathe. They float. Eyes closed. Their faces all so peaceful, so content. Perhaps, they dream some blissful dreams.

I love this face. I know this face. That love is buried deep, lodged like diamonds in my heart. Not Gor. Not Tess. But could be. Might as well. This child is mine. This child is me.

"All the rapt children," Gor breathes, so quiet we almost cannot hear.

We whisper. Though we know the children sleep. How else could we speak? This room is sacred. This room is holy and grotesque.

We stand in wonder. Paralyzed by joy and fear and doubt.

"The fingertips," I say as quiet as the beating wings of moths.

All bare, no marks, no codes. All innocent. Like babes.

Did we too emerge—fully grown, blank face, clean heart, whole but naked—from these peaceful bubbling tanks?

That would change it all. That would undo our memory and shake our story to the core.

In the soft glow, all faces are the same. One floating child opens its eyes. It blinks and smiles and takes its first clumsy underwater breath, and air bubbles stream from its open mouth.

This child is ready to be born.

With strangled shout, we stumble back. My awkward Gor trips backward on some hose stretched out across his path and knocks into some machine, a steel contraption that somehow fuels the tanks.

A siren begins with shrieking noise and glaring lights. We run back the way we came. But pausing at the doorway, we can already hear lockstep footsteps, the thrumming march of Caretakers converging. So we run the other way. All gasping, panting, scared silly. Pushing each other. Stepping on each other's feet, tripping on heels, knocking fists to shoulders as we flail.

We keep on going, though knowing full well our route's reset. But this is it, now, and as good as any other. We'll keep walking 'til we find an edge.

While the Voice echoes in my skull. "You'll find the way. You always do."

We trudge until we reach some steps. A staircase and then a ladder. The path is straight, then curves, then slopes, then spirals. We walk. We climb. We hike. We know that down leads to the ground, so we descend toward earth.

This seems promising. This seems good.

Strange, it's all deserted. Strange, we've seen no Caretakers, no children, since we passed the last cube. No life at all. Like this structure exists almost for itself.

A tunnel. Not like the halls of this megastructure's maze. This tunnel's rounded, like something natural, not like something built. It's wholly dark, no light at all.

"It's all dark now," Tess says.

"Should we keep going?"

"Yes. We're going right," she says. "Don't you see?"

I do see. This is like the world before, the world not built by nanites—no lights embedded, speckled or scattered in what's made. Could be we're almost there. Proud of my smart sister, I grab her hand. "You're right. You're right. Let's go."

"That sound," Gor says. "What is that?"

I hear. I kneel in dark. I pat my grasping fingers against the rocky floor, seeking. It's cold and wet. It's water, flowing in the tiniest trickle at the lowest base of the tunnel's sloped and rocky floor.

"It's wet."

We three feel the walls. Seeking out more trickles. We drip on our dry tongues. We quench some thirst. The water's acrid, tastes of smoke, but still, it helps.

On we walk, holding hands against the darkness.

The waters gather, deepen.

We splash through deep and deeper puddles. Soon, we're slogging through a sluggish creek. Our feet are much damaged by this time, cut and bleeding against the rocky surface. The water washes away the blood.

"Following the water, it feels right," Tess says.

"Like the way we're supposed to go," Gor agrees.

"Like the way we've always gone," I add, though—since when? For what? Maybe people like us, in other histories and all past nows, always following the water, always venturing farther, always seeking out the sea.

The going's slow, feeling along the walls, keeping straight, slogging through darkness, and by now all soaked through.

Rushing water joins us from all directions, everywhere. It's deep, too deep. We're caught. We splutter and choke. I grasp for purchase, but there's nothing there to hold.

"Don't fight!" I gasp through troubled lungs. "Don't fight! Just float."

No choice. I try to stay above the surface. It's cold. It's deep. It's dark. It pulls and yanks. I can't see my sister, nor my Gor. I surrender because it's all there is. Just this.

Just this.

Until we reach the light.

We wash up on an unfamiliar bank. We crawl, almost too broken to move. Our poor hands. Our pathetic knees. We lay on the rocky ground, spluttering and hacking, and covering our eyes.

Because the light is harsh and glaring bright. It bounces aground and bounces back, oscillating between the dingy orange ground and the dreary orange sky.

For the first time in the longest time, I stand beneath the sun.

It's bright and close and hotter than I thought. It makes me squint, and I feel it, like a presence, standing near. A warm wind gusts it nearer. It's almost like it's crushing us, this cruel and brutal heat.

We're battered, bruised, and bleeding. Our clothes all soaked. My sister's hair all sopping, dripping wet. We're not safe yet. We pull ourselves to standing. Wiping running noses. Coughing still.

We search for bearings.

Behind us is the megastructure, looming greater than any city, as I saw in memory duty. And still growing? Can you believe it? Still growing. I see, here and there, knobby protrusions, teetering spires. It's going up and going out, and ever bigger it becomes. Swallowing more world. Gulping everything as it goes.

Stretched between us and the massive gray is a dark flowing ribbon of river.

Ahead are rolling orange hills and massive granite cliffs and flat expanses of barren dust flecked with scrubby brush. It's all the color of terra cotta pots and rocky moonscapes and crimson sunsets over seas, except along the river banks, where the vegetation's thick and flecked with yellow-green.

The air is flat and hot and still. The dust blows, and it smells of dirt and tastes of dirt. Every time I speak, sand and earth float in my mouth. The red clouds huddle low. The smell of burning lingers in the air.

"We're here," says Gor.

We're here?

"It's not like I remembered," I admit, and yes, I'm turning 'round in circles, searching for the world I thought I knew. A city skyline against the blue (this sky is orange or red or gray—or something like all three). The neat green lawns (no blade of grass seen here, though gray and yellow fluff floats in the breeze). The homes. The cars. The neighborhoods where children played. The pieces of it all.

"Nor me," says Gor.

"Or I," says Tess.

But this is it, for sure. This is outside.

A bird wheels overhead, shrieking like a child. A bird—or something like it—its wingspan's wide, like my arms stretched tip to tip. Beaks. And claws. And feathers? I can't tell. Against the too-bright sky, it's just a dark and gruesome shape. This flying creature's joined by others, almost a flock. They wheel and dive. I duck without meaning as if to drop to ground and shelter my tender head. I laugh at myself, embarrassed. Until I see that Gor has done it too.

These birds make no sweet songs. They screech like forks on plates. The sound is awful. Maybe they're threatening us? Telling us this place is theirs and only theirs? Or perhaps, they're dipping in the river. Birds must get thirsty, too.

They spiral honking toward the landscape's edge, disappear into the cliffs.

"Now what?"

"We walk."

We walk. Yes. Until we can't see the labyrinth. Until it's a dot on the horizon no bigger than an ant.

That's the plan.

We walk.

But no matter how far we walk, it looms there. It's too great to escape. It takes up half the sky.

At least we're small.

At least it can't see us.

Or can it?

"I'm thirsty," Tess says. Soon as she speaks, I realize I'm parched too. Tongue dry, lips chapped, throat sore with unwilling-swallowed dust.

"Can we drink the river?" I ask. I'm not afraid. I'm willing to try.

"We almost drowned in it," Gor says. "Like baths. I think I drank some when I capsized. It didn't hurt us yet."

"We'll try," Tess says.

We've been walking in the direction of the river's flow, some distance from the edge. Where we walk, the going's easy. The ground is all flat, smooth rocks and heaps of rust-red dirt. The gray-green shrubs are skeletal and sparse. We trudge along this pebbled desert.

We washed up first in some sandy, beachy spot, but now, we find no entrance point to reach the river's edge. The brush is thick and armed with thorns. This yellow-green thicket rustles with wind or . . . *creatures*? As we get closer, we fear the second. The leaves move with whirring, scraping, clicking.

Chewing? Shudder.

I step into this muggy grove, and all falls silent. No whirring, no scraping, no clicking. Whatever lives inside this bush is awestruck by my footfalls.

This is eerie but okay.

I fight my way through thorns, Gor and Tess behind. More scrapes, more scratches. So I've gone back to the start—my forearms bleed for this.

The brush and herbs I crush smell sharp and clean, like lemons and soap.

From the trees, I feel the weight of gazes. It seems we're surrounded by a hundred bright, unblinking eyes, watching cunning, curious.

We kneel on the rocky bank and scoop handfuls of water to our mouths. It tastes like all of this. The clay-rich dirt. The beating sun. The eucalyptus leaves. It's colder than you'd think and flowing faster than the place where we emerged.

We have no way to carry water with us. We'll stay close to this flow of life and follow where it leads.

As we climb back to the flatland, I hear Gor exclaim in happiness. "A nest!"

We crowd 'round where he crouches: this burrow lined with dead dry leaves, snarls of twiggy branches and that yellow floating fluff. Inside are five sturdy-looking eggs, speckled gray and just small enough to rest within my palm.

"Give me your shirt," Gor says. I do as he commands.

He ties it up into this kind of sack. He's unchallenged expert at storing food in shirts, I'll give him that. Gently, he positions each egg inside this shirt pouch and preps to carry them away.

I fear they'll break into some sticky glop. (I have some thought of this from lost befores: Mom dropping a carton of eggs fresh from the fridge, Bentley swooping in to do his best in cleaning up the mess.) But these desert eggs seem stout and tough.

We walk along, feeling proud. We've quenched our thirst. We've found some eggs, though how we'll eat them remains yet to be seen. We're here. Somehow, it will all work out; we'll make a home, we'll be okay.

But we walk. And walk. And in this endless rocky landscape, it's clear to see there is nothing more than what we've seen. We're on our way to nowhere.

This is all.

"Were our rememberings a lie?" Gor asks. He's gripped by sorrow. I see it in his face. His soft, dear face. His shaggy head. I love my Gor.

"Maybe we're almost there," I reassure. "Keep going."

"Maybe the forest is just around the bend," says my dreamy, hopeful sister Tess.

But we're too tired. We can't keep going. Not any longer.

We flop down on the bare and dusty ground and dig our fingers into crumbly turf, sifting umber sand from hand to hand. The sun is high and all too bright. We pant, sweat. No breeze to cool. We rest ourselves in the meager shade of thorny shrubs.

We nap, all holding hands. Beneath the prickly scrub, beneath the orange sky.

When we wake, it's almost twilight. And cooling fast—good thing our clothes are stiffly dried from all that hot and baking sun. Now what? Now we walk. Pioneers venturing across dead landscape.

"Are we the first?" Tess asks. "How can it be?"

But no traces here of any other world. No rusted hulks of cars, no collapsing ruined buildings, no mass graves. No parks. No swings. No black houses where nightmares first began. No cul-de-sacs, no ice cream trucks, no Kaspar's Play Place, no tin roof rusting in the desert wind.

Against the fading sky, a dark and swirling swarm. This cloud skates the horizon as it coalesces and scatters and forms again.

I know it's nanites. But I hesitate to say, lest Gor and Tess be innocent. I hate for them to fear.

The swarms move faster than our steps. We can't outrun. But I hope and hope it goes the other way. We might still elude, evade. We could find our way and reach our home.

A massive moon rises in a periwinkle sky so close, like we could touch.

Then the stars, igniting one by one. Like memories but more gorgeous still. The beauty takes my breath way.

I feel the cool upon my skin, the ground upon my feet. I feel the world that's bigger than one of us could know, the mysteries we'll never solve, this endless truth we cannot fathom. It's enough. Almost. Not quite. Not ever. But in this moment—yes.

"I love you both," I say to Tess, I say to Gor. "My own Tess. My own Gor. My sister. My brother. I'll love you always. Together, us. Forever. Right? No matter what?"

"No matter what."

"Forever and always."

"This part is true. This part is all."

"I'm tired," Tess says. "Can we sit? Sleep more? I need to rest."

Without waiting for our go-ahead, she flops onto the ground, and we join her, sitting in a half-moon on the sloping hill, and watch the sky grow dark, the stars grow bright. I love it all—the cooling night, the feel of gritty earth, the rolling hills, the wine-dark sky, and all those fierce stars as bright and beautiful as jewels. I breathe deep as I can.

"I'm not quite right," Tess says. "I'm not okay."

"What's wrong?"

She lies back against the sand. "My side," she says. "It hurts . . ." She pulls up her shirt and rests her palm against her side. "Right here. It hurts. Real bad. And getting worse."

I rest my palm where she says. I feel it, pulsing, tender. That swollen sac just beneath the skin, throbbing below her bottommost right rib. Her skin is hot. There's nothing I can do to help.

We hold her hand. "Just breathe," Gor says. "Breathe steady. Maybe it will go away."

She breathes. And whimpers. And moans a bit. We squeeze her hands. We can't think what to do. No medicine. No Caretakers. No Voice. Have we seen this pain before? Maybe? We wouldn't know. We stroke her hair and tell her, *Tess, be strong, be brave.*

It's only getting worse.

We talk to help her think of other things. We recount the stories of our fearsome now, this epic journey only us three children know. Begin with when we found our Tess, watching crimson toucans frolic in virescent trees. We tell this story, like it's myth, passed down generations, like tales of gods of old. We walked across an infinite bridge. We saw where all rapt children are born. We eluded all capture, evaded our prison guards, just well enough to flee. We descended an everlasting staircase. We floated down the dark river that threads its way throughout all things. We made it here. Our home. Not like we remembered. But what is? We're together. No one can steal this memory. We own our story. We're with our loves and finally free.

But my own Tess cries and writhes in pain. She's suffering. It hurts me bad as anything I've ever known. This part? I wish I could forget.

"What's your favorite thing that you remember?" Tess asks through tears, and I remember in my hurting heart that this day we spent, we three, is the only day she knows.

I tell her Bentley. I tell her birds singing raucous in the hour before dawn. I tell her the hammock in the backyard, the summer night, the supermoon. Gor tells about ice cream at the beach—while our empty bellies rumble, sour, growl empty. He tells her running in the surf. We tell her fireworks and fireflies. I tell her blanket forts and safest places and our dog's soft golden fur and softest darkest snout.

Overhead, the stars are going dark.

The nanite swarm blots out the bright. Busy, steady, busy, steady, they turn the sky to dust. The maze is pulling us into itself. The labyrinth swallows us. It always has. It always does.

Tess writhes and cries and then is still.

I kneel over her, touch her face, touch her lips. No breath. I squeeze her wrists. I shake her shoulders. I shout at her. I rest my cheek against her chest. No beat.

This can't be real. This can't be true. I sob against her. Gor squeezes me tight, and he sobs too. It's all my fault. I brought her all this way, dragged her here to die. I thought it didn't happen real. I thought that children only died in memories and dreams.

But she is here and turning cold and breath is gone and heartbeat, too. No more sound, no more speech, and all that spark and sweetness we adored is gone.

"It's all my fault. It's us. We did," I wretch through jagged breath and choking tears and pooling snot.

"The Caretakers can fix her," Gor says, stubborn. He won't believe. "They bring her away . . . they bring her back . . . she'll be okay. All fine. Right?"

"But what if no? What if this is always?"

Another word for time is *always* . . .

"But you'll forget," the Voice says, echoing from every corner of the room. Because the room is here. And all around us. Stinking of ozone. Freshly built.

"You all forget the things you do. You understand now? Why it is and must always be that way? Because if not, your hearts would kill you. You couldn't bear to live."

"But it hasn't always been that way," Gor says. "Right? Because we remember! Other times! Different nows. That world . . ." Angry too. Angrier than I could ever be. His almost over-boiling rage.

"That was before," the Voice speaks soft.

"Before what?"

"Before you traveled too far. Before you reached the edge of human space and saw—something. You should not have seen. You were not meant to see."

"Something like what?"

"Something you'd rewrite everything, all minds, all lives, all history not to know."

"But not us. We didn't . . . we weren't there. In space? Like astronauts? We're just rapt children."

"You're all the same to me."

"Can you bring back Tess?" I demand.

"Yes."

"Now?"

"Later. Soon. Soon enough."

"Why didn't you stop us?" demands Gor, still raging, helpless with fury and anger and loss.

"I get lonely sometimes," the Voice says.

Then the Caretakers are with us, pouring in along the fresh-built hallways. They surround us. They grip us, grab us. They barely even look at us. They don't notice or care this fresh wing of their deathly city is just moments old. They don't notice much, I guess.

Last thing I know is Gor grabbing on to me. And the needle's fierce stabbing in my neck. Then nothing else.

This now is done.

004
(lolo)

LOLO DREAMS OF OTHER THINGS. LOLO WATCHES SCREEN. THE MOON IS made of rock. The moon's suspended in bright stars. Such stars make Lolo dream and feel some joy she almost knows but cannot touch.

Lolo holds two marbles. Marble is orange, marble is blue. These also joy. These also dreams.

The world is a marble that's orange. The moon is a marble that's gray.

The world is also a marble that's blue.

When the Voice calls her code, she comes. Afraid, hurting, sick, sad, but unable not to go. She finds the door. Half-circle, five hollows, five fingers.

Lights flash, and she follows. What happens next? No memory now. She doesn't want. She doesn't like. Something bad.

She lies on a cot. Caretakers—them. She remembers now. She hates. They stink like rot. "Does it hurt?" she asks. They won't answer. Never do. She remembers now, too. Lolo speaks. Not them. Not they.

Bright lights. Bare belly. Cold gel. No tears. All numb.

Lolo's terror is pure and bright and turns to rage. How could they do this? This nightmare? This deepest ugliest hell?

They cut, they reach. Extract clear sac.

They can't. They must be punished. She'll fight them hard. If she could just remember long enough to fight.

Caretakers turn together, moving like one creature with more bodies than it needs. Backs to her. They fill syringe.

Lolo thinking blurry, but through murky thoughts, she holds the rage. She tests the strap. Does she always test the strap? She must, every time. Countless times, perhaps. She tests again.

It gives. It's loose. It's not secured. This time. Only?

Lolo holds deathly still while the Caretakers turn back and rummage nasty-fingered at her side. Inject syringe into the wound.

They turn away, again; they need the spray that heals.

Quicker than lightning, Lolo reaches out. Grabs the scalpel lying on the science cart. Tucks up her sleeve. Then back as she was before. With fierce instrument hidden to herself. Cold metal nestled near her flesh.

She'll do what with it? She doesn't know. Some power it holds. This talisman, she thinks. A voice whispers, *Grab,* so she grabs. She holds. She'll hide. She'll keep. Until she remembers what she needs to do . . . one step. Next step. She'll fight.

Needle pumps. It's done. All gone. A pulse.

This takes too long. Her thinking's slow. It comes and slips away just like the ocean tides.

Some later, Lolo finds this scalpel in her sleeve. She's bleeding, cut. Her own Gor is there. He wraps his shirt to stop the blood. She walks, fast as she can. Before forgetting. She climbs in bubble. She hides this scalpel under bunk. Thinks fast as she can think (never fast enough). Pulls back the cloth Gor wrapped. Sticks fingertip against the cut. Smears with blood. With bloody fingertip she traces an arrow on the wall; the arrow points to blade.

I wrote, she thinks. *This first. I'll change . . . I'll change it all.*

This now, the blade lies safe beneath the bunk.

§

Desirina Boskovich's *short fiction has been published in Clarkesworld, Lightspeed, Nightmare, F&SF, Kaleidotrope, PodCastle, Drabblecast, and anthologies such as* Aliens: Recent Encounters, The Apocalypse Triptych, *and* Tomorrow's Cthulhu. *Her nonfiction pieces on music, literature, and culture have appeared in Lightspeed, Weird Fiction Review, the Huffington Post, Wonderbook, and The Steampunk Bible. She is also the editor of* It Came From the North: An Anthology of Finnish Speculative Fiction *(Cheeky Frawg, 2013), and together with Jeff VanderMeer, co-author of* The Steampunk User's Manual *(Abrams Image, 2014). Find her online at www.desirinaboskovich.com.*

BROKEN EYE BOOKS

NOVELLAS
Izanami's Choice, by Adam Heine
Never Now Always, by Desirina Boskovich

NOVELS
The Hole Behind Midnight, by Clinton J. Boomer
Crooked, by Richard Pett
Scourge of the Realm, by Erik Scott de Bie

COLLECTIONS
Royden Poole's Field Guide to the 25th Hour, by Clinton J. Boomer

ANTHOLOGIES
By Faerie Light, edited by Scott Gable & C. Dombrowski
Ghost in the Cogs, edited by Scott Gable & C. Dombrowski
Tomorrow's Cthulhu, edited by Scott Gable & C. Dombrowski

Read books.
Stay weird.
Repeat.

www.brokeneyebooks.com

twitter.com/brokeneyebooks
facebook.com/brokeneyebooks

CPSIA information can be obtained
at www.ICGtesting.com
Printed in the USA
BVOW03s1244310717
490712BV00003B/162/P